Joe's

LATE GREAT AMERICAN
DREAM

A NOVEL

Other Novels By Jon Christopher

Meanwhile There Were Dragons
Moving At The Speed Of Time
Somewhere Out There In The West

A TRAVELING SHOES PRESS BOOK

LATE GREAT AMERICAN
DREAM

A NOVEL

JON CHRISTOPHER

TRAVELING SHOES PRESS
PO BOX 332
Pioneertown, CA 92268

Joe's Late Great American Dream
ISBN# 978-1-732-92052-1

First Edition | 2020
Edited by Jean-Paul L. Garnier and Mark Leysen
Book design by Jon Christopher

- Dedication -
Stephen Joel Jensen
Gregg and Sheri Pasterick

c

Contents

f

Foreword
(Frank Capra On Acid)

L et us begin contrarian: There are looming reasons why I may have no business writing this foreword for Jon Christopher.

First, I am more akin the noir/pre-Beat stranglehold where everything has to be inherently doomed for it to be interesting. In fact, as I look at all the books on my shelf right now, they all reluctantly carry this same burdensome weight, boasting their predestined curses loud and proud. These traits have given enormous (mis)guidance to my own trajectory as a writer and for better or worse, my personal life.

But that's exactly one of the reasons why it feels so good to be writing this for Jon – people wouldn't *expect* it of me. It feels defiant to be writing the intro for an author who possesses the rare guts to make the reader feel good. What a fucking concept!

Let me back up. The first time I read one of Jon's books (*Moving At The Speed of Time*), an extraordinary thing happened. I was at a pivotal segment in one of my favorite crime writer's best-selling books, adrenaline squirting out of my pores, *stress-reading*, seeing just how bad things could get for the conflicted protagonist. I was determined to finish the book that day, after I came back from Jon's release party for *Moving At The Speed Of Time*.

Well, I didn't finish the crime book until months later. It was intercepted by the out of left field Court Jester whimsy of Jon's book. It was like a fresh breeze coming through my window, ushering the suffocating, dead-air of my noir fetish out the front door, like a smiling mouth exhaling a goooooood hit of primo weed. I saw how anxiety-ridden the best-seller was making me. Did I really need more confirmation that the world was a sad, selfish, desperate place where death is the only sure thing? That feeling was already long rooted in my DNA, and probably wasn't going anywhere. But I began to see the noir book as repellent compared to Jon Christopher's. Here was a writer who was actually *uplifting* me. And as a result, I could not put the book down. Instead, I finished *his* book that day.

Inevitably, I returned to darkness. But I was forever altered by Jon Christopher and what was possible – even acceptable - in a modern novel amidst our seemingly dead-end times. His stories start with humble beginnings of the every day Joe (especially this one in your hands) getting swept up in kaleidoscopic adventures that are rooted in the everyday, yet fully committed to the fantastical. But the strangest aspect of Jon's books might be the fact that these wild tales always culminate into happy endings where no one really gets too hurt, though maybe a couple heavy lessons learned along the way. He's like Frank Capra on acid. He'll often break the Fourth Wall, and talk directly to the reader – a disembodied consciousness making you feel like you're in on the magic as well.

He has such a command over the craft of "matter of fact," that it often feels like he may be putting one over on you. That's because he often is, much like the sneak-ups Vonnegut always tested us with. But it's never at the expense of a universal sentimentality, the way he weaves disparate yet simpatico pop-culture archetypes together, if not people from your own neighborhood. He cross-hatches and stretches it out to unseen horizons until it feels like they were born grooving inside us all along, intertwined.

Jon's books aren't only limited to us humanoids, either. He often ties in otherworldly creatures to give it an apocryphal, conspiracy theorist's slant. Which makes me think: Jon's books should be translated into every single language on Earth - that way, if the all-knowing aliens really do eventually come down here, maybe they wouldn't perceive us as the ruined civilization we have convinced ourselves we are?

— Gabriel Hart, author of *Virgins In Reverse & The Intrusion*

i

Intro

The lights came up in the arena. The E Street Band had just ripped through the two opening numbers and the crowd was getting warmed up by the high energy of the Boss and his crew.

"Good evening, Long Beach," shouted Bruce Springsteen to the crowd. His voice came up at the end of "Beach" with a lilt.

"We're so glad to be here tonight!" The crowd went wild.

"Are you ready to be entertained?" he yelled and the crowd roared back its approval.

"Are you ready to be ENTERTAINED?" Bruce's voice had an added urgency. The crowd roared back even louder.

"Are. You. Ready. To. Be. TRANSFORMED?" The crowd went wild with applause.

"1... 2... 3... 4..." Bruce counted off the next song, the house lights went down and the E Street Band, firing on every cylinder kicked into *Born In The USA...*

1

The U. S. of A.

Once upon a time there existed a mythical land called the United States of America. Everyone was free and goodwill between men and women was the common social thread. There was equality and justice for all. The crime rate and unemployment rate were extremely low. The people were strong and industrious and family-owned companies paid their workers high wages. Home ownership was as common as air. The children were obedient and loved their parents.

Everyone in the whole world wanted to move to the U.S. of A. because it was the best country that had ever existed on the planet. When the crowds at sporting events chanted, "U.S.A. is number one," they meant it because it was true. Everyone knew it was true.

That was decades ago and the state of America had fallen into disrepair. Joe knew it. Everyone knew it. There was a grayness of depression that permeated the atmosphere like a wet blanket. Joe sat on the back step of the small apartment he rented on the westside of Long Beach. His left arm was in a cast from an unfortunate accident several weeks earlier. He was vaping large clouds of smoke and looking through his social media news feed on his phone.

It was Saturday, June 2nd, and the skies of Long Beach were gray with what the locals called "June gloom". Music was coming from inside Joe's apartment. Not surprisingly, it was the Boss on the stereo. Bruce Springsteen's classic album *Darkness On the Edge Of Town*, which was Joe's favorite record, was playing with the volume cranked up high. Today was the fortieth anniversary of album's release and Joe had read an article in *Rolling Stone* about it earlier, so he had to play the record, of course. Joe was a long-time fan of the Boss. The Boss and U2 were his favorite rock acts, hands down.

Joe Smith had been born after the mythical land of the U.S. of A. disappeared and was replaced by the broken-down country familiar to everyone nowadays. He was born eight years after his favorite Springsteen album came out. He didn't need anyone to tell him he had missed out on the good times. Like most people, Joe couldn't really put his finger on when this mythical America had flourished, but like everyone else, he believed it existed once, long ago.

The grayness, the clouds of vaped smoke, the stories on his social media news feed, the slight fuzziness from last nights' drinking all muddled Joe's brain like an oatmeal mush. This is the subject of our story: Joe Smith, age 32, with a square jaw, a muscular frame and a shaved head. Joe stood about five feet nine inches tall and was considered fairly attractive by most women.

Joe's last serious relationship had been several years earlier with a girl named Debbie. The relationship had lasted four years and the two had almost got married. Unfortunately (some would say fortunately), two weeks before the ceremony Joe found out that Debbie was having an affair with his best friend Tom. The wedding was canceled. Joe had not yet recovered from the betrayal and was a bit leery about getting into another relationship, as you might imagine.

In Joe's dreams there was the perfect woman out there somewhere waiting to walk into his life, he could picture her in his
mind – her blonde hair, her cheerleader voice, her love of Bruce
Springsteen... but all his dreams: the good job, the nice house, a
loving wife, and an all-American kid – none of these things were
even on the horizon.

Then there were the other dreams, the secret dreams Joe shared
with no one else. One was the dream where he was recognized as a
great writer. This wasn't close to happening because Joe never
showed his short stories to anyone, no one except his ex-best
friend Tom. After reading one of Joe's stories Tom had jokingly
told Joe not to quit his day job. Joe had taken what Tom said seriously and now he was rather gun-shy about sharing his writing
with anyone.

Joe also had another dream that wasn't getting close to coming
into reality, and that was to be an astronaut. He dreamed about it
often, ever since he was a child. The lure of the unknown fascinated him, and the vastness of space represented the ultimate unknown. A person might think that Joe wrote science fiction based
on his astronaut dreams, but he didn't. He wrote about the everyday things he encountered, the news of the day and the people he
met, with a kind of homespun American realism.

The day job that Joe was encouraged not to quit was a supervisor position at a place called AZRecycle in Wilmington, just
north of Long Beach. Joe's work mostly consisted of driving a
forklift all day, moving bins of recyclables around, and managing
the current crop of laborers.

There was a smell like sour milk and stale beer that Joe
couldn't get out of his nose after eight years working for AZRecycle. Some nights Joe dreamed in Spanish after spending all day
with his crew of laborers. Joe still had a soft place in his heart for
the workers who came and went in his life, and hadn't grown cal-
lous as had most of the management.

Bill Diamond, Joe's boss, had put up a big sign in the recycling yard that said, "Welcome to America, Speak English". Joe, along with everyone else ignored the sign and spoke Spanish. Bill was a shameless racist and called everyone in the yard "Jose". Lately he wore a red hat that said "Make America Great Again" and the bumper stickers on his SUV expressed his support of the NRA, the President, and, of course, GO U.S.A!

Joe thought Bill was an idiot, and now, on this June gloom Saturday he was glad he didn't have to deal with Bill or his job for the weekend. As he vaped large clouds of smoke, the coffee he had finished earlier started to kick in and his thinking ramped up a notch.

Joe thought about several new workers who had started that week. Before they had immigrated to the United States, Roberto and Xavier had come from Nicaragua. They had both been professionals, in management. Roberto was a recent arrival and was especially optimistic about the opportunities available in his new country. Xavier had been here longer and was more realistic about an immigrant's possibilities in present day America.

The rest of Saturday afternoon Joe spent writing a short story inspired by Roberto's enthusiasm, a quality Joe felt missing from his life. Joe titled the story "With Blinders On" and the story had a tragic ending full of lost love and regrets. After a quick edit of the tale Joe printed out a final copy of the story and filed it away in the wooden filing cabinet his mother had given him years earlier. Joe wasn't counting, but that was the fifty-second story he had written in the last five years.

2

The Greatest

It was late in the evening when Joe went out to his usual spot on his back step to vape for a while. He enjoyed a cold Stone IPA while he listened to the ever-present sound of police sirens in the air. The sky had an orange glow, as usual, and Joe could see the constellation of Orion, the only stars really visible from his back yard. Joe wondered if there was anyone out there, on planets circling those distant stars.

Joe had put U2's *Joshua Tree* album on the stereo. He always put on *Joshua Tree* when he finished a story. Writing a new short story left him content and peaceful, satisfied. Now the songs of U2 rolled on in the familiar order as he vaped and enjoyed sips from his beer. He thought of his friends back in Salt Lake City, where he had gone to high school. Back then he had been a pretty righteous Mormon. He was named after the founder of Mormonism, Joseph Smith. His buddies had all been into U2 more than Bruce Springsteen, so Joe had grown into an affinity for the Irish band, but they weren't the Boss, and the Boss was a solid American. He was a guy from the neighborhood.

Joe had been born in New Jersey before his parents moved the family to Minnesota when he was four. So far Joe had lived in

New Jersey, Minnesota, Iowa, Utah and California. Sitting in west Long Beach on the coast of California, Joe was about as far west as he planned on going.

That night Joe had a dream. He was smoking cigars with the President of the United States on top of an impossibly high building. The two were admiring the scenery when the President looked at Joe and said, "You know, this is the highest point in human history, the greatest." and he clinked his champagne glass with Joe. At the base of the building everything was decayed and crumbled. When the glasses clinked the first floor turned to powder, then the second, then the third and so on. The building didn't collapse, it just dissolved from the ground up.

"Go U.S.A!" said the President, as he waved his cigar around at the glowing city lights. Then, like in a cartoon, the building dissolved out from under the two while they hung motionless in the air. After an endless moment, they dropped like stones. Joe woke up just before he hit the ground.

Joe lay in bed for a while before drifting off into sleep again. The next day the dream stuck with Joe as he went about his Sunday chores. He played *Darkness on the Edge of Town* again, twice while cleaning and washing dishes, trying to get other thoughts going through his head besides the dream.

Joe had his Sunday casuals on — a sleeveless Bruce Springsteen T-shirt and a pair of tight-fitting shorts that he thought of as showing off his muscular body. The shorts were striped with colors that made one think of Miami. He wore a pair of flip-flops that had waving American flags on the soles. To top off his outfit, Joe had tied an American Flag bandana on his head. Thus attired, he headed off to the store to get groceries for the next week.

Joe shopped weekly at Ralphs on Fourth Street, on the east side of Long Beach. It was his favorite grocery store, even though it was a short trek across the city. He had been shopping there for the last few years and some of the checkers would remember his face when he went through the line – that always made him feel good. There was something comfortable about the familiarity. Joe loved the small town feel of being recognized, like he fit in his place.

Familiarity had its good points. Take Gallagher's pub for instance. It was on Broadway, a few blocks from Ralphs. Joe ate at Gallagher's often and met there with a group of some-friends-of-a-friend on most Thursday evenings for Happy Hour. Joe kept going on Thursdays because he had grown used to these people – they smiled and said "hi" when he showed up. Sometimes he had a good conversation, but mostly they were all into bike riding, much more than Joe was. None of them were Springsteen fans. Joe kept going because he hoped the girl of his dreams might show up some Thursday, you never know. He went for the hope and the fact that it was comfortable and familiar.

Familiarity also has its down side. The sense of familiarity had kept him working at a job going nowhere. The familiarity kept him in his rather run-down westside apartment. Familiarity was what had kept him with Debbie and why he almost married her.

Joe drove slowly and took the long way home from the store, down Ocean Boulevard and past the beach, through the downtown, and up several side streets to his apartment. The sky was still gray from the June gloom and the light of the afternoon caused Joe to want to close his eyes from the diffused glare. Lots of people were out in the park along Ocean. Joe noted a man standing on a crate preaching. He had seen the guy several times before. What he didn't see was the sign on the side of the crate that read "357 days until the end of the world".

3

Cindi Wilson

When Cindi Wilson left Bakersfield, she didn't plan on ever going back. Everything she had hoped for: a great guy, a nice house, and kids someday, had evaporated one night when she came home early from her job at Ralphs grocery store to find Shane, her fiancee, in bed with her second-best friend. It had been an awkward and horrible moment.

The breakup was swift.

Cindi was further humiliated to find out during the breakup that Shane had slept with nearly half of her girlfriends. Everyone knew about it but her. She withdrew from her social circle and went into a deep depression for a few months until she decided what to do.

Cindi's cousin Kim lived with her husband in Whittier and Cindi had visited them a couple of times. Kim encouraged Cindi to leave the toxic Bakersfield world that was doing nothing but depressing her and come live in Whittier. Cindi agreed with Kim and requested a transfer at work. There was a job available in somewhat-nearby Long Beach, so Cindi asked to be transferred to that store, anything to get out of Bakersfield, and quickly.

In a few short weeks she had moved into an apartment on Third Street in Long Beach, a short bike ride from her new job at Ralphs on Fourth Street. The building had eight apartments all facing a central courtyard. Cindi's new home was apartment C, which really pleased her, because, you know, her name started with a C.

Cindi, who was an avid bike rider, was thrilled that her new city had taken a decidedly bike-friendly approach – bike lanes and bike paths were abundant. She often rode her pink beach cruiser down to the park by Ocean Boulevard.

Even though she was born in Ohio, Cindi was a California girl, through and through, and fit comfortably in her tan skin and long blonde hair, which she often wore pulled back in a pony tail. Just barely twenty-seven, she had a friendly face and the warm smile of an ex-cheerleader. She had been a cheerleader for over a decade, from junior high all the way through college. She was also a Springsteen fan. A really big Springsteen fan.

Cindi was also a smart woman and had maintained a 3.98 grade-point average all the way through college. She was empathetic and sensible and she had a good heart for discerning situations. She was really thrown off when she had missed all the signs with Shane and his cheating ways. She was, of course, smart enough to realize that there had been a certain amount of willful blindness on her part. That was a mistake she wasn't planning on repeating. As a matter of fact, she wasn't particularly interested in finding love now, or looking for it. Most of the guys who asked her out she politely turned down. In spite of this, Cindi, being naturally friendly, quickly made new friends wherever she went in Long Beach. Being a bike rider it was inevitable that she would eventually run into Ricky Santiago.

Ricky had noticed Cindi before, several days earlier at Ralphs, so when he saw her coming down the bike path towards him he stopped his bike and waited for her to pedal closer. Ricky held up his hand to get her attention, and Cindi stopped as she rode up to him.

"Hello stranger," said Ricky sticking out his hand.

Cindi shook his hand and answered back in her friendly way, "Hello to you..."

Ricky, Cindi soon found out, was the go-to guy in Long Beach when it came to bikes and bike activism. He had emmigrated from Brazil when he was a child and had an easy-going charm about him. His charm was one of the reasons Long Beach had turned into such a bike-friendly city. With his boyish dimples, he charmed everyone he met whether he tried or not, and the city council had not been immune to his easy smile and heart-felt speeches in favor of bike lanes and bike paths.

Cindi was quickly falling under Ricky's spell when another girl rode up. The girl was strikingly beautiful. Ricky gave the girl a kiss when she rode up to where the two had been talking.

"Suze, this is our new friend, Cindi," said Ricky to the girl.

Suze had long dyed red hair with severe bangs. She wore a bikini top and shorts. It was easy to see that most of her body was covered with tattoos, elegant lacy designs that covered her arms, torso and down her legs. She eyed Cindi up and down, obviously wondering who this new girl was talking to her boyfriend.

"Hi," said Cindi giving an awkward little wave.

"Where are you from?" asked Suze, not the least bit interested in being friendly, "You don't look like Long Beach." As friendly as Ricky had been, Suze was cold.

"Hey, c'mon Suze, don't be like that," said Ricky with a twinkle in his smile.

"I'm from Bakersfield," responded Cindi, wondering what would make her look like she was from Long Beach.

"What an armpit," replied Suze, "good move getting out of there." Suze's attitude seemed to be thawing out just a bit. The three talked on the bike path for another ten minutes with Suze getting progressively warmer until they all got out their phones and became "friends" on social media.

Cindi rode away slightly infatuated with Ricky, which was the first impression many girls had when meeting him. Suze knew it, and kidded Ricky about it as they rode off down the bike path. Ricky was madly in love with Suze and took the kidding lightly.

The next Sunday morning, on Cindi's day off, she got a text from Ricky asking her to go on a group bike ride that afternoon. Cindi joined the biking group and about twenty bikers rode from Long Beach down the coast to Seal Beach for a late lunch and beers. Naturally, in her friendly way, Cindi was quickly accepted by the group and after a couple beers she was pouring out the sad story of her and Shane to Suze and a girl named Meghan. Suze and Meghan hugged her and they all cried a bit. They went outside and each had one of Suze's cigarettes. It was the third cigarette Cindi had ever smoked. It was a serious bonding moment. Before the day was over Cindi had over a dozen new social media friends.

Cindi had, by this time, scrolled through Ricky and Suze's social media news feed and noted that they seemed to visit the pub up on Broadway every week. She wasn't surprised to get a text from Suze on Wednesday asking her to join them Thursday evening at Gallagher's for their weekly Happy Hour gathering. Unfortunately she had to work on Thursday evening but she texted back she would try and make it the next week.

4

Joe's Dream

The glow of Ricky's charms had long worn thin on Joe. He had been going to Ricky and Suze's Thursday Happy Hours for nearly two years and he was tired of hearing about bikes, bike lanes, bike accessories, bike advocacy, bike trips, etc. His friend Steve, who had first brought him to Happy Hour, had moved to Portland, Oregon and none of the people in the group had really become close friends.

Joe let the conversation drift around him and felt himself pull back from the group. He sipped on his beer and decided that tonight was his last Happy Hour for a while. After all, the only reason he kept coming was because it was the familiar and regular thing to do each week. That, and the hope that the girl of his dreams would show up some day — but she hadn't.

As he sat there he looked around the table for what might be his last time. He was surprised how many people at the table now existed in his short stories, filed away in his wooden filing cabinet. There was the story about Annie and her escape from Oakland. There was Clifford and his bike trip across America. There were the stories about Ricky and the city council, Suze and the car show, Ben and his secret CIA past, Nick and his attempt to make home-brewed beer – each person had shared some story with him that had been transformed into a piece of fiction.

Now a new story was forming in Joe's head and it included disappearing. It was about new beginnings. He knew it was going to be his story and it would begin on a night like this. On a night when the mood was in a certain way, and the faces around him seemed a little distant, like they were already receding from view.

Joe paid his bill, downed the last sip of his beer and ate the last couple french fries on his plate. Then he got up and said goodnight to the group. There was a round of so-long and see-you-next-week from the people at the table. Joe headed out to his car parked down the block.

Fifteen minutes later he was home where he cracked open a fresh beer. It was only eight and he had a few hours left before bedtime. He started writing a new story, the one he had begun in his mind at the pub that evening. In Joe's story he abruptly changed his life, moved to a small town, got a different kind of job, and met the girl of his dreams. The tale was left unfinished when Joe went to bed a little after midnight. Joe had titled the un-finished story "Joe's Dream".

5

Disappearing

Joe couldn't get his new story out of his head. All day Friday, while he worked, little bits of the tale fell into place in his mind. But even more than the content of the story, the idea of leaving for the unknown was starting to get under Joe's skin and gave him a traveling itch. Sometime around two in the afternoon Joe decided he was going to quit his job – not today, but the time was coming. He was going to think about his options over the weekend and then see what next week would bring.

That evening Joe fell asleep on the sofa watching a baseball game. While he slept he had a long dream about being an astronaut. Endless amounts of time were spent floating in the void of space. He traveled to a far distant planet and met strange aliens, one of whom strongly resembled Ricky. Joe seemed to move from one ship to another, always heading out into the vastness.

Joe woke up after two in the morning covered in sweat. There was some commercial for a psychic playing on the TV and Joe clicked it off. After going to the bathroom and grabbing a fresh beer from the fridge Joe sat back down on the sofa. The astronaut dream was still present in his thoughts. Moving, traveling, going – the growing need to head out into the unknown was overtaking him. He got out a map of Southern California and spread it out on the coffee table. While he sipped his beer he thought about different places on the map. *Riverside? Redlands? San Diego? How about a small town like Idyllwild in the mountains, or Big Bear? How about the hi-desert near Joshua Tree, Wrightwood or Landcaster?*

Joe looked closer at the map of the Joshua Tree area. *What about Joshua Tree?* It had been years since he had gone camping in Joshua Tree with his friend Steve. He had really enjoyed that trip and was impressed by the desolate beauty of the area. Joe sat back on the sofa and closed his eyes, taking a deep drink of his beer. *How about a road trip in the morning,* thought Joe. Joe took another sip and agreed with himself that a road trip sounded like a good idea.

Joe thought for a while if there was anyone he could invite to go with him, but couldn't think of anyone. Steve was in Portland and Tom turned out to be a dickhead and he hadn't talked to him in several years now. Other than that his friends list was lacking. Thinking about his lack of close friends made him feel untethered and strangely free. *No one will miss me if I just disappear,* he thought.

He went outside to vape for a while. Besides the police sirens the air was still and quiet. The orange glow of the Long Beach night obscured the stars, as usual. Joe looked up and thought about the idea that tomorrow night he'd look at the stars in the dark skies of Joshua Tree. The idea made him truly happy. *Baby, you were born to run,* he told himself, paraphrasing the Boss, and he took a huge inhale from his vaporizer and blew out clouds of smoke. Joe downed the last of his beer and headed to bed.

6

Mike And Leslie

Joe slept until ten the next morning and didn't get on the road until after one. It was the 30th of June, a Saturday, and there were 329 days until the end of the world. It was over a hundred degrees in Joshua Tree when Joe arrived at the National Park Visitor Center around four that afternoon. Joe looked around the Visitor Center for a couple of minutes, left, and crossed the street to the Joshua Tree Saloon.

When he got to the saloon it was fairly crowded. To the right of the door there was a big, round booth with just two people sitting in it on the far side of the table. Joe asked if he could join them, for lack of any other place to sit. The two people, a couple in their mid-sixties, said they'd be honored, so Joe slipped into the booth. After a short wait Joe had a cold twenty-two ounce IPA in front of him and he was starting to get to know the couple he was sitting with; Mike and Leslie Wilson, retired gypsy innkeepers. Mike was sipping on an ice tea, and Leslie was slowly nursing a glass of white wine. When Joe's beer arrived they all toasted to Joshua Tree.

Mike, it turned out, was an amateur astronomer. The two had moved to Joshua Tree because it was a dark skies community, which is great for looking at stars. They had recently retired from over thirty years of traveling around the country doing short term management for motels and bed-n-breakfasts. Leslie had a number of tales to tell of various places they had run. Their stories got Joe's imagination running and he grilled them about how they got started doing this, he had never heard of such a job.

After a couple of hours, delicious food had been eaten, several drinks consumed, and the conversation had ranged from UFOs, to boulder climbing, to fall colors in the Appalachian mountains, to space travel and the various constellations, peppered with numerous tales from Mike and Leslie's gypsy adventures. Mike and Leslie didn't do social media, so they exchanged phone numbers instead. There was some talk about the possibility of barbecuing the next day and handshakes were exchanged, along with a warm so-long.

Joe went outside to the smoking section to vape while he finished the last of his beer. It was hot in the late afternoon sun, still near a hundred degrees. While vaping, Joe looked up local places to stay on his phone. After calling a few places he cussed at himself for not making arrangements before he left Long Beach. After his fifth call he finally found a room at the Best Western in nearby Yucca Valley. Not exactly the rustic desert experience he had been hoping for.

On his way to the Best Western Joe stopped at the Stater Brothers in Yucca Valley to buy some beer and food for later that evening. Joe wandered the grocery store, still slightly buzzed from the beers he had earlier, and his mind started thinking about how much he liked grocery stores. He thought about his weekly trips to Ralphs on Fourth Street, and how comfortable he felt there. The more he thought about it the more he realized that maybe a job at a grocery store was just what he needed. The thought made Joe extremely happy and a sense of calm and purpose came over him.

This could be the new plan for a new job, maybe in a new town, maybe in Yucca Valley? Why not? Maybe this Stater Brothers? Joe almost forgot why he had come into the store, the thought was that mind-blowing. After a moment he remembered what he was doing and grabbed a six-pack of beer, a deli sandwich, some chips and ice cream.

The sun was setting as Joe came out of the grocery store. Venus was visible in the west and the first stars were starting to come out. Joe stood in the parking lot for a moment to enjoy the last of the color in the clouds before it faded and then he remembered he had ice cream which would be melting in the ninety-five degree heat. He got back on the road.

Joe drove to the Best Western where he had a pretty standard room on the second floor. Beer, sandwich and ice cream went straight into the refrigerator and Joe laid back on the bed and closed his eyes to rest for a moment. In minutes he had fallen deeply asleep. He dreamed about being an astronaut again, working in a grocery store in space. Twenty minutes later his cell phone rang, waking him up. It was his friend Steve. It must have been ringing for a bit because the call had gone to message by the time he grabbed the phone. Joe listened to the message. Steve wanted to come down for a visit and wanted to know if he could stay on Joe's sofa.

Joe called Steve back immediately.

"Hell yes!" was Joe's enthusiastic response to the idea of Steve visiting.

Joe and Steve talked for the next half hour. Joe told Steve all about his new plans to work at a grocery store, about his astronaut dreams and about the dream with the President and the dissolving building. Steve caught Joe up on his current situation. Steve had met a girl named Irene who was a local musician and bike advocate in Portland. He was thinking about asking her to marry him. He felt like he needed to get away for a few days to sort out his thoughts and that's why he wanted to come for a visit.

"Come on down and stay as long as you want," said Joe.

"How about the weekend after the 4th of July?" asked Steve.

"Perfect. How about arriving on the sixth, it's a Friday and I'll be off from work for the holiday weekend?"

"I'll order plane tickets tomorrow. Is it okay if I stay a week? I wanted to go to Thursday Happy Hour and see everyone."

"Stay a week... stay two and we'll come camp out here in Joshua Tree. I'll take time off from work. I have several weeks of vacation time built up."

"I'll miss Irene too much if I stay two weeks." Joe could hear the grin on Steve's face through the phone and suddenly he realized how much he really missed his only true friend – and fellow Bruce Springsteen fan.

After the phone call Joe went downstairs and outside the hotel. The lights of the parking lot obscured the stars a bit but there were so many more to be seen than in Long Beach. Joe stood in the smoking area for a while, vaping and staring up at the sky, thinking about the many worlds that must exist out there in the vastness. Looking out, Joe felt like he was standing on the shores of the great unknown, and something out there was calling him to go, to travel to the stars.

"Baby, you were born to run," Joe said to himself and fist pumped the air with his right arm for emphasis. Of course, Joe knew that was just a dream, like so many other dreams in his life, something that was constantly out of reach, beyond his grasp, and no matter how hard he tried he just couldn't seem to get there.

7

BBQ With The Wilsons

That night Joe dreamed long dreams of driving, endless hours on highways – crossing country, crossing cities, crossing deserts. Going and going with no destination in mind. Sometimes he was a hitchhiker, just a passenger, sometimes he was driving the car. Joe woke up exhausted the next morning, an exhaustion that even the first two cups of coffee with his continental breakfast couldn't overcome.

When Joe got a text from Mike suggesting a barbecue at 3:00 he had mixed emotions. Leslie had mentioned something the day before about their daughter visiting from Long Beach, and "wouldn't they have a bunch in common?" To Joe this sounded a little too much like match-making and he didn't feel like getting set-up. He was hoping for a love that happened naturally. Mike sent a follow up text – their daughter couldn't make it, she got called into work or something, but the barbecue was still going forward. Relieved, Joe texted back that he'd be there. Mike sent the address and Joe sent back a smiley emoji.

After checking out of the hotel Joe had some time to kill, so he drove aimlessly around Yucca Valley to get the feel of the place. He wound up in the old town area and went to some local gift shops. He had a delicious BLT for lunch at a cafe called Frontier and drove up Pioneertown Road to the old movie sets from the 1950s he had read about online. He drove back through Pipes Canyon and saw some of the most beautiful hi-desert imaginable. It looked exactly like the old westerns. Not knowing where to go he followed the twists and turns of the road and eventually found himself at Highway 247, Old Woman Springs Road. Joe was lost at this point, but a quick check for directions on his phone had him heading back to Yucca Valley and the Stater Brothers – best to arrive at the barbecue with supplies, like beers, burgers and buns.

Mike was playing *Nebraska* by Bruce Springsteen when Joe arrived and hearing the album made him feel right at home. Mike and Leslie greeted Joe with a hug when he arrived. Something about being at their house felt like coming home.

Mike offered Joe a pipe with some marijuana. Mike had started smoking pot in the last few years and was an enthusiastic proponent of the herb. Joe said thanks as he received the pipe and took a little hit. Joe rarely smoked pot and he didn't want to get too stoned.

"Cindi got me high for my first time," said Mike.

"Cindi?" asked Joe.

"My daughter. She looks so innocent you would never know how much she likes to smoke the herb. She got tired of my bad moods and insisted I try it one day." Mike pointed to several pictures on the bookshelf. They were of a fresh-faced teenager in her cheerleader outfit. "She's a smart one," he said, and then he took another big hit from the pipe.

Joe started to feel the marijuana effect him and began marveling at his surroundings. Mike and Leslie had such an interesting place, full of souvenirs from their many adventures in gypsy inn-keeping. Joe walked around the living room asking Mike about the various objects. With the tie-dyed wall-hangings and the number of dream-catchers, rattles, guitars, tarot cards decks, crystal balls, wizard hats and more, Joe felt like he was in a hippie museum.

Mike was silently amused by Joe's curiosity about his various knick-knacks. He liked this guy. He couldn't help but wish his daughter could meet a guy like Joe. He shook his head as he thought about the recent relationship fiasco Cindi had just gone through. *Poor kid*, he thought. Like any overly concerned father Mike was sure he was somehow responsible... *maybe we moved too often while Cindi was growing up.*

Leslie came out of the kitchen into the living room and asked Joe if he wanted a beer, and wasn't it time to get the barbecue going? "Absolutely," they responded, and the two of them followed Leslie through the kitchen where drinks were procured, then out the back door to the patio. Joe asked if it was okay if he vaped, which didn't bother Mike or Leslie. Mike even took a small vape hit just to see what it tasted like. It tasted like honey and caramel.

Mike lit the barbecue and after a short while the burgers were cooked perfectly. Mike had barbecuing skills. The afternoon rolled into sunset and soon the stars appeared. Leslie encouraged Mike to get out his telescope and several hours were spent checking out various objects in the sky. Joe told them about his dream of being an astronaut, which he hadn't shared with anyone, except Steve, since he was a kid. It was after 11:00 when Joe started talking about hitting the road.

"We have a guest room..." Leslie suggested.

"No, but thank you kindly. I've got work in the morning."

"Are you good to drive?" asked Mike.

"I'm great. I'll just put on some Bruce and haul it back to Long Beach."

And that's what Joe did — after goodbye hugs, he hopped into his car, put the CD *Born To Run* on the stereo, and by the second song, *Tenth Avenue Freeze Out*, he was already on Highway 62, heading west, back to Long Beach.

8

The Calling

Jeremiah erased the number eight from the blackboard on the side of his prophet cart and wrote a seven. Everyday Jeremiah subtracted one from the number on the blackboard and wrote a new number. 327, the current number, was the amount of days left until May 25th of the next year, otherwise to be known as "the end of the world". Jeremiah's sign on the side of his prophet cart read in full – "327 days until the end of the world".

Jeremiah's prophet cart was his soap box on wheels with a built-in, battery-powered PA system. Jeremiah hauled the cart around Long Beach, where he would set-up in various parks to announce the coming end of the world. The Almighty had given him this project several years earlier and he was doing his best to carry out God's orders.

It was Sunday night, around midnight. Elsewhere, in Joshua Tree, Joe had recently left Mike and Leslie's house to head back to Long Beach. In a different elsewhere, many light years from Earth, there was a fleet of spaceships from a planet named Estes-Sol on their way to our world, but we'll get to that in a minute, first let's talk about Jeremiah.

Jeremiah was a prophet of the Almighty, not in the delusional way as might be expected in our modern world. He really heard from The Man Upstairs – not constantly, but on a pretty consistent basis. Jeremiah used to be a regular kind of guy but that was over twenty-five years ago, before God Almighty had called him to be a prophet. Being a prophet is not a choice a person makes, it's a calling, it's something that happens to a person that changes them completely.

Jeremiah's calling had come one afternoon while he had been camping by himself in the forest of Idyllwild in the San Jacinto Mountains. Jeremiah had intended on it being a week-long spiritual retreat but it had been unfruitful so far, to say the least. God, it seemed, was as non-existent at his primitive camp site as a hot-shower, replaced, instead, by large mosquitoes, and lots of them.

Jeremiah, who was at a cross-roads in his life, had gone to the mountain to find God and to get some answers. His daughter, Catherine had recently died from a long battle with cancer and his wife, Terri, who was grief-stricken, had left him.

Two years ago life had been so perfect, and then Cathy's illness had struck the family like a hammer. Jeremiah had returned to his childhood faith in God and learned to spend long hours on his knees praying for his daughter's life. He felt strongly that God would heal their daughter and told Terri repeatedly that everything would turn out all right.

Well, it hadn't turned out all right and Terri felt a tremendous amount of anger at both God and Jeremiah. Terri left them both soon after the funeral and Jeremiah slipped into a deep depression. One thing had led to another and here Jeremiah was, on the mountaintop giving it one last try and then, if this failed, who knows? Maybe it was time to just hang it up...

Jeremiah had fasted for three days before he gave in and started eating from the small supply of food he had brought along. His legs and arms were covered in mosquito bites. He gave up on prayer and the next day he drove into town to buy some beer, more food and mosquito repellent.

Now he was back at his camp site, covered in mosquito spray and sipping on a cold one after eating a delicious deli sandwich. For the first time all week Jeremiah felt relaxed as he reclined in his camp chair with a full belly and a beer in his hand. The light was good and from his campsite he realized he had a great view down into the valley below which had been obscured by clouds since he arrived.

"Jeremiah," a voice came from behind his head. He got up and looked around. There was no one there and after a minute he sat back down again, puzzled.

"Jeremiah," said the voice and this time from seemingly in front of him. Jeremiah wasn't sure if he was imagining the voice – was it in his head or was he actually hearing a voice, because there wasn't anyone there that he could see.

"Jeremiah, I have heard your prayers," the voice spoke again. Jeremiah decided the voice was definitely coming from outside his head.

Ah, thanks, it's about time, thought Jeremiah. This was an extremely weird thing going on and the hairs on his arms and legs were standing up.

"You're welcome," replied the voice, "People are coming to visit you soon. Share what you have with them."

"What, who?" said Jeremiah out loud. There was no answer, just the sound of the wind through the trees.

A few minutes later a car came driving into the campground. It was an old car, a beat-looking sedan in need of a new muffler. The car drove slowly along the road until it reached Jeremiah's camp spot. The car paused for a moment before pulling into the empty spot next to his. The engine shut off with a shutter and a cough. Jeremiah watched the car with interest. He couldn't see inside and wasn't sure what to expect but these were obviously the people the disembodied voice was talking about minutes earlier.

A slender girl, barely twenty it looked like, got out of the passenger side of the car at the same time a long-haired guy with a scar on the side of his face got out of the driver side. *Drug addicts*, was the first thing Jeremiah thought. The two had a dark look about them, something sinister and criminal. The guy looked over at Jeremiah and pointed at him. It felt like a dagger struck Jeremiah between the eyes.

"Do you have any more beer, mister?" said the girl as the two walked towards Jeremiah.

"Ah, yeah," replied Jeremiah and he got two bottles of beer from his cooler.

"Thanks, mister," said the girl, as the guy popped the caps off the beers.

"I'm Hank and this here is Allie," said the guy. Hank had a southern twang to his voice.

"I'm Jeremiah," replied Jeremiah, sticking out his hand to shake with Hank.

"I know," smiled Hank as he shook Jeremiah's hand, "and I'm really sorry about your daughter Cathy."

Jeremiah was completely thrown off by hearing Cathy's name mentioned by a total stranger.

"How do you know about Cathy?" responded Jeremiah angrily. This really touched a nerve.

"Oh, I know a lot about you. Dig this, you have seventeen mosquito bites on your right leg."

Without counting Jeremiah knew this stranger was probably right. He wasn't sure what to do and he felt completely disarmed. He gave Hank a funny look and didn't say anything.

"Almighty God has sent us to find you for a purpose, but first let's enjoy these fine beers," Hank took a big swig from his beer.

Jeremiah motioned to the picnic bench and they all took places around the table. Hank started talking to Jeremiah about his ex-wife, Terri, and their separation, assuring him that their marriage was, indeed, over. The Man Upstairs had new instructions for Jeremiah and a change in life plans. Jeremiah listened, feeling both irritated and intrigued by Hanks bold assertions. Every so often, while Hank talked, Allie would raise one hand towards the sky, look up and quietly say, "Praise Jesus".

After the beers were finished Jeremiah offered his guest fresh ones but they declined.

"We have important business to attend to," said Allie with an unexpected seriousness.

"God has called you to be a Prophet," said Hank with equal seriousness, "and we're here to anoint you for service."

Allie got a small bottle of olive oil out of her purse. Jeremiah was confused and started to protest.

"There is no use protesting Jeremiah, this is God's will for you," replied Hank, "just sit there and we'll do all the work."

Hank and Allie stood up and walked behind Jeremiah. Both of them laid hands on Jeremiah's head and Hank said something in another language. Jeremiah felt the hands lift off his head and in a few seconds the unexpected sensation of olive oil being poured on his hair. Jeremiah was really about to protest but instead his mind burst with an explosion of light and love. He opened his mouth and out came words in a language he didn't recognize, but then he knew what the words were, and they were praising the Creator of the Universe for the perfection of His creation, and for mosquitoes. And at that moment Jeremiah meant everything his strange words were saying.

Jeremiah must have been lost in a spiritual ecstasy, because by the time he opened his eyes again Hank, Allie and their car were all gone. He hadn't heard them leave. The forest was quiet and Jeremiah had a sense of peace he had never experienced before. Olive oil was dripping from his head onto his shirt. Jeremiah sat for quite a while at the picnic bench reveling in the wonder and the vibe of the moment.

And thus began a long and strange twenty-five year journey which brought him to 327 days away from the end of the world. Along the way Jeremiah had seen numerous miracles; he had watched food multiply so many times it's not funny, he often turned water into beer, and occasionally he healed the sick.

And then there were the conversations with God. Jeremiah had tried to write down each one, but they happened almost weekly and rarely when it was convenient to stop and make notes about what he was hearing. Still, Jeremiah had enough words from God to fill many notebooks. The Almighty is rather long-winded it turns out, as could be expected of a divine entity not constrained by time and space. A number of years ago God started talking to Jeremiah about the end of the world.

9

Ships From Estes-Sol

Elsewhere, as I mentioned a few pages back, there was a fleet of spaceships on their way towards Earth. These ships were all from Estes-Sol, a planet orbiting a star in the Cygnus constellation. The ships were traveling in a series of hyper-jumps at many times the speed of light, they planned on arriving sometime in April of the next year. They were, in a way, in a race against time.

Their interest in planet Earth went back thousands of years. The aliens from Estes-Sol look exactly like humans on Earth, and about one percent of one percent of Earth's population came from Estes-Sol. One could think of Earth as an interesting social experiment run by the elites from Estes-Sol. Who are the high-level people pulling the strings of the world? You guessed it, it's aliens from a planet light-years away. And now that the world was coming to an end, a fleet of space ships had been sent to rescue the Estes-Sol immigrants and their offspring and bring them back to their home planet.

The people of Estes-Sol are called Solarians, they are an angelic race, meaning they are immortal and have free will. For some reason, on Earth they lose their native immortality, but they also experience reincarnation, which is unheard of on their home planet. Many of the royalty of the planet Earth are reincarnated Solarians, as are many of the financial elite of the planet.

On board the lead ship in the fleet was a fearless warrior. The ship's name was *Constant Wind* and the warrior's name was St. John of Sol – he commanded the whole fleet. Every hyper-jump was coordinated by St. John. The jumps lasted several minutes and they happened every few day. There were limits to how far the ships could travel at one time. The jumps put a lot of wear and tear on the ships and time was required to calculate the next jump. Following this relentless schedule, the fleet had been underway for several months. While the ships traveled through sub-light speed, St. John had the crew perform numerous rescue drills to ready them for the eventual day when they would arrive at Earth. When that moment arrived the rescue plan had to work like clockwork, there would be no time to waste.

St. George of Anthem was the commander-in-charge of the rescue operations. St. George was a hearty soul with a great thirst for beer. Fortunately, Estes-Sol produces the best beer anywhere in the galaxy and when the Solarians headed out into space they took micro-breweries with them. Anthem, by the way, is the second largest city on Estes-Sol. You probably don't need that information for this story, but if you're ever traveling that way you would want to know. Another bit of useless information – IPAs were first brewed by Solarian immigrants.

10

Dynasty

With 327 days left until the end of the world, Nathan Dynasty was busy running the world-wide corporation called Black Shield, one of the oldest corporations in the world. Black Shield was the world's banker to the bankers. No one, except maybe the Queen of England, was richer than Nathan Dynasty.

Nathan had no idea that there were only 327 days left to financially manipulate the world as his family had been doing for hundreds of years. If he had known he would have redoubled his efforts to make even more money at the expense of the world's population, he was weird that way.

Nathan was the descendant of some Estes-Sol aliens who had immigrated to the planet hundreds of years ago. Most of the offspring of the Dynasty family were reincarnations of the original alien immigrants. Reincarnation had not been good for the consciousnesses of the aliens from Estes-Sol. The souls of the Dynasty family had turned grotesque with each reincarnation, and now, a dozen generations down the line, the family had mutated into something dark and evil. Nathan couldn't really help himself as he made life miserable for billions of people, his soul was horribly bent that way. I'm not excusing Nathan for his perverse and evil ways, but there was a reason he was no good, you know what I mean?

The history of the Dynasty family could be the subject of a whole book, which it is, actually. For the whole story look up the book *Dynasty: A Dynasty – The Unauthorized History*, if you can find it. The book, put out by a small independent press, is really hard to find. Nathan and his family like to keep a very low profile and rarely did they allow stories of themselves to appear in the mainstream press. Because they own practically every news outlet and press in the world through their various corporate holdings, this wasn't hard to do.

"The world is a business," it has been said, and to Nathan this was exactly the truth. His family had been working on a plan for centuries to transform the world and its people into the image they had in mind. And that image, simply put, was totalitarian globalization – a single world corporation ruled by the Dynasty family. The plans included many wars, lies, and manipulations to accomplish their goals. By financing every side of every war they controlled the outcomes to fit their overall plan. "The best way to control the opposition is to lead it ourselves," Nathan often said, quoting the one-time communist revolutionary and former Dynasty employee, Vladimir Lenin.

A person might think this is some conspiracy theory, and it was indeed a conspiracy, but no theory, it was just simple business thinking going on. Secrets are the lifeblood of large corporations and by design, conspiracies are necessary – small groups of people get together to figure out ways to manipulate the larger world into buying their products and services. If these plans were known to the general public they could never pull off the lies and manipulations needed to succeed in the larger world of corporate titans. The corporate titans, the super-corporations, the multi-nationals, these were the chess pieces Nathan and his family moved around on the world's playing board as they slowly and patiently worked towards their goal.

The plan had been instituted by Julian Dynasty in 1548 in Frankfurt, Germany. Julian, who was a visionary and a genius, envisioned a completely interconnected world where monarchies would be abolished and the common human would live like a king. His vision was altruistic and humanitarian. Julian truly wanted Earth to reach its highest potential. Julian was a first generation immigrant from Estes-Sol and wanted his adopted planet to reach the heights of civilization that Estes-Sol had achieved.

As each generation replaced the previous one, the plan became nastier and more sinister. This continued for many generations until the plan had mutated into one of pure greed and power.

There were other entities that had interests in Earth too, and their plans didn't agree with the Dynasty plan. The most well-known of these entities was God Almighty, who had completely different plans for this delightful little oasis in space. Before the whole place had been corrupted by commerce and civilization, it had been an extremely nice planet full of life and magic. God liked to visit often, assuming an animal form, and spending long periods of time living among his creations. It was a good life, until the Solarians stumbled across Earth.

God thought that he had hidden the planet pretty well, but the Solarians were super-smart. God had, of course, created them that way, and with free will, millions of years earlier. Free will being what it is, the Solarians had used their opportunity to develop a world-wide civilization and reach out to the stars.

As I mentioned in the last chapter, God had created the Solarians as angelic beings with immortality, a decision he regretted and didn't repeat when he built Earth. On Earth he used a different kind of life process. Life, or consciousness, is, after all, energy and is neither created or destroyed. God envisioned life on this planet as living in a series of biological containers. They would be born into a body, live and then die and then the consciousness of that life would be inserted into another biological container to continue the process. We call this process reincarnation and it has been going on for millions of years. Meanwhile these reincarnated consciousnesses of Earthlings were growing into mature cosmic beings, and would someday be ready for immortal bodies. Reincarnation worked better for native Earthlings than it did for the consciousnesses of the Solarians.

It was a grand yet cautious plan which the interlopers from Estes-Sol had now made a complete mess of. So God was pulling the plug on the Earth project and planning a complete reset. The reset was coming in 327 days. At least, that is what The Guy Upstairs had told Jeremiah.

11

Cosmically Speaking

The Solar System is a beautifully designed place. The planets rest in precisely defined orbits that create beautiful patterns as they spin through the cosmos. Each sphere in the Solar System hums and vibrates with its own song, sending out their songs to each other, to the Sun, and to all the living creatures upon the face of planet Earth. The songs, the vibrations, cause changes in the creatures on the planet. Depending on the location of various planets and moons in the Solar System, the mix of vibrations change, creating a seemingly random pattern of moods, energies and thoughts. Humans are deeply affected by these changes in vibration, but most people are hardly aware they are going on all the time.

Aristotle was constantly aware of the vibrations of the planets and moons. He was an astrologer, from a long line of astrologers, and was a direct descendant of Nostradamus. He was, in fact, Nostradamus reincarnated, but neither he nor anyone else knew this. The consciousness that was once the famed prognosticator had chosen to return at this moment in time because of its cosmic significance. Who wants to miss the end of the world?

Aristotle had a psychic shop on Sunset Boulevard in Hollywood. A large sign sat on top of his shop that read, *Aristotle the*

Astrologer – Psychic To The Stars. Many A-List, B-List and lesser Hollywood stars had all had private consultations with Aristotle. He wasn't impressed by celebrities, they were more messed up than most people, but they sure paid well.

Aristotle had recently been contacted by the First Lady's secretary. The First Lady was deeply concerned about her husband's welfare. Politics, especially on the international level, was a dirty and nasty line of work, and she had a number of troubling dreams where she saw the President get shot. The President had made a lot of enemies since he had come to Washington, so her fears weren't too far-fetched. The First Lady wanted a list of the most dangerous days for the President, astrologically speaking, so his schedule could be adjusted. And it had to be kept quiet, very quiet. If word got out to the press that the White House had consulted an astrologer the press would have the proverbial "field day" with this one.

It was during his investigations for the First Lady that Aristotle stumbled across an intensely troubling date, May 25th, in the coming year. The cosmic alignment of the planets and moons was unlike anything he had come across before. The conjunctions between Mars, Saturn and Jupiter were completely disastrous, and nearly every planet would be in retrograde motion. There were other astrological factors involved, but professionally speaking, it was a cluster-fuck of monstrous proportions. Aristotle sent his report to the White House with May 25th red-flagged as a highly significant day. He made a note of it in his private diary.

12

Aristotle's Premonitions

Aristotle was at home with his partner of exactly seven years, Jose Ibis Esteban St. Marie. Jose was five years younger than Aristotle and came from a wealthy Spanish family. He was a Leo with his moon in Libra. This was, of course, an astrologically perfect match for Aristotle Valencia.

Aristotle was a huge fan of the late-entertainer Liberace. Aristotle wore a large white wig infused with golden glitter. He painted his face to highlight his clear blue eyes. He wore robes adorned with mystical symbols. He was quite a sight when you saw him out of context, like at the supermarket, fully made up as Aristotle the Astrologer.

At home, Aristotle was more subdued in his personal style and would let his long hair down. Today he was lounging around the pool in the backyard watching Jose splashing and diving, playing Marco Polo with several friends that had come by for a barbecue. It was the seven-year anniversary party for Aristotle and Jose. They were going to announce their engagement later that evening.

As Aristotle lounged in the backyard watching Jose frolic with their friends and sipping gin, he vaped on a pen full of cannabis oil that contained 90% THC. It was powerful stuff. Soon he was napping, drifting in and out of sleep in a delightful fashion. While he slept he had a dream.

It was a warm day in the dream, clear and pleasant. Somehow he knew it was May 25th. Suddenly the sky seemed to catch fire. Meteors filled the sky, streaming down from space as large burning chunks of rock. Everywhere was death and destruction. In his dream he saw Jose die and he woke up in a panic. Jose was leaning over him, dripping water from the pool, about to wake him with a kiss. Aristotle reached out and grabbed Jose's head and pulled him close for a long kiss. Unsettled by his dream, he held on to Jose, afraid to let him go.

13

The Spoon Bender

Elsewhere in the Los Angeles area, was another psychic, Claude Lyons. Claude did not have a psychic shop and had never given a reading for a celebrity. Currently he worked at a part-time job taking phone orders at a local pizza joint in San Pedro – it supplemented his social security check.

Claude was in a deep funk. The previous year had been a descent into depression as he felt life on the planet Earth coming to its conclusion. He had been having nothing but world-ending dreams for months, and Claude knew to trust his dreams. He had always enjoyed life, strange and difficult as it was, and was sad to see it coming to an end. Claude used to be married, but his wife of twenty-five years, Nicole, had died quite some time ago. He had several sons and daughters who would visit him every so often. His nearest daughter lived in Los Angeles.

Claude dreamed about the future and he could bend spoons with his mind. Neither talent brought him much joy. Claude had learned a long time ago that people neither wanted to know the real future, nor did they want their spoons bent. Most people preferred you leave their silverware alone and keep quiet about the future.

Claude had May 25th noted in his planning book for the next year, the day was circled in red. The date had shown up in so many dreams that he knew it was a highly significant day, quite possibly the last day on Earth. He planned on having a party on May 24th with all his close friends and family, that would be on the Sunday of the Memorial Day weekend.

Claude was also religious. He had grown-up Catholic and had not strayed from his roots in spite of his psychic abilities. Every day he said prayers to Mary to intercede with Jesus Christ to prevent the destruction he saw coming. He nearly wore out his prayer beads with the force of his petitions. In the great cosmic scheme of things Claude's prayers did very little but produce hot air. But it gave Claude some satisfaction that he was doing something, whatever he could, to avert disaster.

Claude had seen Aristotle's commercials on late night television. Aristotle was dressed up in all his make-up and robes in the commercial, sitting behind a crystal ball. In the crystal ball flashed numerous famous faces, and the background was filled with storms and lightning. The voice over said, "During life's storms, it's important to know there is someone you can go to for advice," and then the words, "Aristotle the Astrologer – Psychic to the Stars" would flash on screen followed by an 800 number. The commercial would play over and over on late night TV, interspersed with commercials for used cars and prescription medicines. Claude thought that Aristotle was a fraud.

One night Claude decided to call the 800 number. Claude had consumed a number of whiskey sours and was feeling feisty. He had a few questions for this Aristotle character. After the typical recorded message about all calls being monitored for training purposes a polite woman came on the line.

"Aristotle the Astrologer, Psychic to the Stars, my name is Bethany, how may I help you?" said the woman on the phone. Bethany was a staff psychic, one of twelve, and as she told Claude, all the staff psychics were trained and overseen by Aristotle himself, and no, Aristotle was not available for phone consultations.

"Does Aristotle know about May 25th?" Claude asked, his speech slightly slurred from the whiskey.

"May 25th, hold on just one minute sir," and Bethany put Claude on hold. For weeks they had been getting calls about May 25th, it seems this date was on a lot of peoples' minds even though it was over three hundred days away. More than a few amateur psychics had contacted Aristotle to see if there was a reason this day seemed so important. Aristotle had a big sign posted in the phone room full of staff psychics stating that all calls referring to May 25th were to be directed to him personally. Aristotle was collecting as much information as he could about the day.

Aristotle had already talked to over a dozen psychics and heard a variety of reports about the day, none of them good. There were visions of meteor showers, asteroid strikes, Earth exploding, visits from planet Nibiru, nuclear war and cosmic ray disasters. Several callers believed the Sun was going to explode. More than a handful of callers suggested that Jesus was going to return on May 25th.

After a short wait Bethany came back on the line, "Aristotle would like to call you back and ask you a few questions. There will be no charge for this personal service. Can I get your phone number and a time you can be reached?"

This is more like it, thought Claude. He gave Bethany his name and number and said he would be available the next evening. Bethany assured Claude that Aristotle would call around seven.

14

Dream Consultant

The next evening Claude was waiting for Aristotle's call. He sat at his kitchen table with the phone sitting in front of him. He stared at the phone. He had a whiskey sour – a double in a tall glass – on the table next to the phone and he kept taking small sips while he waited. At seven o'clock, on the dot, the phone rang.

"Hello, Claude Lyons? I'm Maria Montello, Aristotle's personal secretary, could you hold one moment for Aristotle?"

"Thanks, sure, I'll hold." replied Claude.

After a few minutes a male voice came on the line. "Good evening Claude, my name in Aristotle."

"Pleased to meet you, I've, ah, seen your commercials," Claude was surprised that he was a little choked up talking to a famous person.

"Got to keep the roof on the place," replied Aristotle.

Claude laughed, nervously. "Right, business..."

"So, you called about May 25th. What significance does this day hold for you?" Aristotle got straight to the point.

"I've been having dreams about that date for over a year."

"Really? What happens in your dreams? Is there a reoccurring theme?" Aristotle's intuition was telling him this was an significant person on the phone.

"I believe it might be the end of the world," replied Claude, and he took a big gulp of his drink, finishing it off.

"How does it end?" asked Aristotle.

"Don't you know?" replied Claude.

"As a matter of fact I do," responded Aristotle, "but I've been getting so many calls about May 25th that I've been calling people back to find out what they see coming."

"Well, I've seen a number of different world-ending scenarios, the dreams always keep changing. I've seen the planet explode and I've seen it turn into a snowball."

This was just what Aristotle had heard from a number of callers. It seemed the world was ending, if these psychics could be believed, it was just a question of how.

"Does Jesus show up in your dreams?"

"Nope, no Jesus and no rapture. In some dreams it seems that aliens showed up and saved a number of people."

"Aliens?" This was a new one to Aristotle.

"Yeah, just the other night I dreamed that all these spacecraft arrived and saved a bunch of people before an all-out nuclear war started."

"Really?" Aristotle was making notes, "how many times have you dreamed this and how recently?"

"It's been a reoccurring theme, the aliens, I mean," replied Claude, "you know, maybe once a week for the last few months."

"What do the aliens look like?" Aristotle's curiosity was peaked.

"Like humans. They have ships that look like flying marbles. Really small. Then they expand to the size of a building, just like that, into large luminous spheres or bubbles."

"Mr. Lyons, this is fascinating, could I meet you in person? I see that you have a local phone number, would it be possible for you to come to my office on Sunset Boulevard? I'll pay you for a consultation."

"You'll pay me?" Claude was surprised by this offer, pleasantly surprised. He could stand to make a few extra bucks on the side. They made arrangements for Claude to come by Aristotle's shop the next Saturday, around noon, and the phone call ended. Claude sat back in his chair, and looked up at the ceiling to stretch his neck. That had gone much better than expected. Claude fixed himself another whiskey sour, a double, and thought about what next Saturday would be like. He expected he'd have a dream about it that night.

When Saturday came, Claude was at Aristotle's Sunset Boulevard shop at a quarter to twelve. Maria Montello, a tall, fashionably dressed Italian woman, showed Claude into Aristotle's outer office. The bookshelves were lined with copies of Aristotle's many books on astrology and the tarot. There were star charts on the walls and an old fashioned neon sign that read "Fortune Teller" over the door to the inner office. The fortune teller sign was buzzing and flickering, slightly overpowering the soft music playing through speakers in the ceiling.

Aristotle opened the door and invited Claude into his inner office. The lighting was subdued except a spotlight that shone down on a crystal ball sitting on a round table in the middle of the room. There were five chairs around the table and Aristotle motioned for Claude to sit in one of them.

"Thank you for coming," started Aristotle, "will three hundred dollars be sufficient for a one hour consultation?"

Claude did his best to hide his surprise. "I'm sure that would be fine, you know, pay for my gas and all."

Aristotle asked Claude a bunch of questions about his psychic abilities. Claude bent a half dozen spoons and shared several example of his dreams in the past which had been very accurate. They talked for a while about May 25th and Aristotle explained about the number of people who had contacted him about that date. He showed Claude his star charts for the day and how all the alignments were bad. Then he offered Claude a job – Dream Consultant.

Aristotle offered Claude one hundred dollars a day as a retainer, and two hundred for every dream report, whether it was about May 25th or not. Aristotle believed in paying his psychics well because it produced better results. Claude accepted the job on the spot. Aristotle handed Claude an envelope containing three hundred in cash for the consultation and shook his hand. He walked Claude back up to the front office where Maria Montello got his personal and tax information, explained the dream report procedures and gave him a bunch of paperwork welcoming him to Aristotle Inc.

15

Biological Clock Ticking

Steve called Joe one evening, several days after Joe returned from the desert. The trip was off. Steve couldn't get the time off from work after all. Joe tried his best to hide his disappointment. Joe had already taken time off from work for the next week and had been making plans for stuff they could do. Steve also had other news – Irene was pregnant. They had just found out the day before. They were going to get married at the courthouse in a month. Joe wished them well, hung up the phone and sat thinking for a while.

Joe felt his biological clock ticking and he thought about how he better make some changes soon if he was going to participate in the great American dream. He thought about the Stater Brothers in Yucca Valley. They weren't hiring right now, but Joe's intuition told him that maybe he had a future there. Joe also thought about the Ralphs on Fourth Street. Maybe he should try to get a job there first.

Joe shook himself out of his thoughts and got up to go outside to vape. He grabbed a cold one from the refrigerator before heading out his back door. Joe left his beer on the step and wandered around his backyard vaping. A neighborhood cat had made his backyard its home and now came over and wrapped itself around Joe's ankles as he stood staring at the sky.

Suddenly strange lights appeared in the sky! Joe's heart started beating extra hard as a burst of adrenaline shot through his system. The lights, the UFOs, floated silently several hundred feet over Joe's apartment. They were otherworldly looking. The lights all seemed to burn with an inner fire and Joe tried to take several pictures with his phone but they didn't turn out too good.

After a couple of minutes watching the dozen lights drift across the sky Joe realized what he was seeing. The lights were flying Chinese lanterns. He had been to a wedding once where they had lit similar lanterns and watched them fly away into the night. Joe wondered what was the occasion for the lanterns, usually it was a wedding or something but it was a Wednesday night. Of course there was nothing on his social media about it, Joe checked.

In a few minutes the lanterns drifted out of sight and the sky returned to its usual orange glow. Joe retrieved his beer and took a seat on the step. *Weddings*, he thought and he wondered if he'd ever have one of those. In his mind he saw a picture of his dream girl and wondered if she really existed.

Someone once told him that if he was meant to be with a person then that person's feet were headed his direction, and his feet were headed in their direction, and it was just a matter of time until you met. The person who told Joe this had suggested that you bless the person coming towards your life, and in that way you cause blessings in their life before they even meet you. Joe wasn't sure he believed this but said a little prayer of blessing each time he thought of his dream girl, just in case, not that Joe was any good at praying.

Like seventy-two percent of Americans, Joe believed in God Almighty, but this general belief in God did little to impact his personal life. This belief in The Man Upstairs had been instilled in Joe at an early age as a Mormon, reinforced over and over growing up. Tied to this belief was the idea that this nebulous Almighty God favored America over all other countries, and by default, Americans were a blessed and chosen people. Joe never gave this any deep thought, it was just taken for granted. "God bless America," as they say.

Now, it's debatable, to be sure, about whether God blesses America, but it is beyond question that the Dynasty family had blessed America for generations. This was, of course, because America's existence and its rise to prominence was important to the Dynasty plan. Now the time had come to destroy America to create the right situation for the final step in their long-ranged plans.

Joe had once read an article about Nathan Dynasty, Black Shield and the Dynasty plan to take over the world. The article had been on a conspiracy website and Joe had *almost* believed the story, but it was just too crazy, the thought that one family could be pulling the strings of the whole world. Of course, it was this kind of disbelief that the Dynasty family counted on to shield them from scrutiny.

How did the Dynasty family do its string pulling? Simple things really, and most of them had to do with banking and the tremendous wealth Nathan could apply to situations needing his attention. A simple rise in the price of oil would have a number of rippling effects and could even cripple a nation.

There were many, many corporations that Black Shield owned, and those corporations owned corporations, and those corporations owned companies all over the world. Goods, services and products could be denied to a country on Nathan Dynasty's whim. But Nathan didn't have whims, he had plans, concrete plans, and those plans involved the growth and destruction of any nation necessary to serve the grand Dynasty objectives. Here's a list of countries that have resisted the Dynasty plans in the last forty years: Afghanistan, Iraq, Syria, Libya, Iran and North Korea. Most countries don't resist pressure from Nathan Dynasty very long before they give in to his demands or war is threatened and destruction soon follows.

As Joe vaped on his back porch he was, like most people in the world, pleasantly unaware of these international intrigues. Mike Wilson paid attention to Nathan Dynasty and his activities by going to certain conspiracy websites, but Leslie never wanted to hear about it. Cindi Wilson, like her mother, couldn't care less about someone named Nathan Dynasty.

Jeremiah knew about Nathan, much more than most people because God had told him a lot of inside information. There are many unpleasant details about Nathan's private life we won't get into, but it had to do with secret ceremonies, multiple murders and strange rituals. Nathan, along with the rest of the Dynasty family were truly nasty people.

16

The Late Great Hour

For those who like their Christian scripture served with a large helping of scary end-time prophecy there was probably nothing better than the 11:00 PM broadcast of Dr. Charles Harmon on the Christian Broadcasting Channel. Thousands of people regularly tuned in to *The Late Great Hour* to listen to the doctor of theology and get their socks scared off.

Dr. Harmon's favorite subject was The Tribulation, the seven year period that would be controlled by the Anti-Christ, in conjunction with the The Beast. The Doctor could talk about the horrors of the coming tribulation until you pissed yourself with fear. Charles seemed to get a special pleasure in watching his studio audience react to his prophecies.

"There will be large guillotines built to slice the heads off of those that don't take the number of the Beast," Charles would pause for affect, "but those that take the number of the Beast will burn in hell for all eternity." He would pause again and let the horrifying dilemma be fully realized.

"Are you ready to face the guillotines for Christ?" Charles often used references to guillotines because it really made people squirm.

Dr. Charles Harmon had been doing the tribulation routine for nearly fifty years. He had written a number of books about the end times but he was best known for his first book called *The Late Great World*. It went to the top of the *New York Times'* bestsellers list for months back in the 1970s. No doubt a large number of people like to be scared shitless. Selling scare stories to the large Christian audience, not to mention the American public in general, was extremely profitable and now, fifty years down the road, Charles had so perfected his spiel that he could do it in his sleep.

Now, if you're wondering if Charles believed any of what he talked about I'd have to pause and think about that for a moment... the answer would be yes and no. On one hand Charles was a true believer in the Bible, the book of Revelation in particular. On the other hand he was a guy with several big houses, a jet airplane, and lots of cars – doing his routine because it paid well.

Charles' theology was known as "post-trib". He believed the church would have to go through the tribulation before Jesus returned. End Time theologies are defined by when Jesus is going to return. Some people believe Jesus returns and raptures all the Christians before the tribulation times, these people are known as "pre-trib". Some people believe Christians will go through half the tribulation period before the rapture happens, these people are called "mid-trib". Charles had found that the "post-trib" model sold best.

Charles had the future all mapped out. Along with his many books he had diagrams, charts, and timelines. He had videos with CGI enhancements that showed what the seven year reign of the Anti-Christ would be like. They were terrifying, of course. They contained lots of guillotines.

"The Beast will make everyone get implanted with RFID chips. Without a chip you won't be able to buy food," Charles liked to talk about a future where everyone will be micro-chipped and numbered. Years ago he used to say that people would be bar-coded in the future but his predictions had changed with the new technology. "If you have no RFID chip then it'll be off with your head."

Joe had tuned into *The Late Great Hour* several weeks earlier. Joe was just flipping around the stations and thought he had found an interesting movie to watch. It was a short preview clip from Dr. Harmon's movie called *Anti-Christ: Seven Years Born In Hell*. The video scared the crap out of Joe, which was what it was intended to do. There were, of course, many scenes with people being dragged off to guillotines. Rivers of blood flowed and behind the killing was the maniacal Anti-Christ, who was empowered by the Beast and by Satan himself. Joe streamed the complete movie and watched it until two in the morning. He had nightmares the rest of the night. Since then the end-times had been in the back of his mind.

17

Jacques Lapin

Jacques Lapin was an independent international terrorist based in Montreal. He hated Black Shield, with a passion. He had spent the last twenty years formulating a plan to take down the international corporation. If you remember the numerous bank bombings of the late 1990s and early 2000s, that was Jacques Lapin. That was just his early, crude analog attempts to disrupt the international bankers. Since then Lapin had turned to the digital underground as a computer hacker to bring down Black Shield through quieter, backdoor means.

For more than two decades Lapin had always kept more than three or four steps ahead of Interpol, the FBI and the CIA. He had developed a series of false identities that hadn't failed him yet. Every couple years he would go through facial reconstruction surgery to fit his latest identity. The only thing he wouldn't let the plastic surgeons do is reduce the size of his enormous ears. In his latest incarnation he had grown an impressive beard as Samuel Livingston, fossil collector. Using this identity Lapin moved effortlessly around the world in spite of his ears.

Jacques was a follower of Dr. Charles Harmon, he watched the *The Late Great Hour* religiously. In some ways, Lapin felt like he was doing God's work, bringing down the international banking cartel known as Black Shield. Lapin had gathered and read thousands of Black Shield internal memos by hacking their message servers, and he was convinced of their evil and inhuman intentions.

Lapin had not found his way to Nathan Dynasty's personal message server, yet, but it was the continuous target of his hacking attempts. In Jacques Lapin's mind Black Shield was The Beast that would enable the rise of the Anti-Christ. And if Dr. Charles Harmon was even close to accurate, the world should be seeing the rise of the Anti-Christ any time now. Lapin felt like he was in a race against time to prevent this from happening.

Late one July night Jacques launched an internet attack on the International Monetary Fund and succeeded in bringing down their network of computers. The attack was merely an inconvenience for the IMF, but the world's financial markets were thrown into turmoil for a couple of days. Lapin's plan was to create instability in the markets through repeated attacks and brought down the IMF computers several more times over the next two weeks. Doubt is poison to the financial system, and the repeated attacks started to sow seeds of doubt.

After a series of seven successful attacks, Jacques went quiet for a while. All the international law enforcement agencies had increased their look out for the hacker or hackers responsible for the attacks, and he thought it was best to disappear. So as fossil collector, Samuel Livingston, Lapin went out to do some field work and collect some fossils.

Meanwhile, on August 1st, Dr. Charles Harmon was injured in a shooting incident at the TV recording studios. The security guards had wrestled the assailant to the ground and he had been arrested by the local police. Hugo Von Schmidt was the assailant and he told the police he had attacked Dr. Harmon because he had been molested by the doctor many years earlier, as a child. Hugo's only regret is that he wasn't a better shot. After news of Hugo's reasons for shooting the doctor hit the airwaves seven other men, including a prominent TV actor, came out and told their stories of being molested by the doctor years earlier.

The Late Great Hour was canceled the next day.

Jacques was outraged when he read the news while out in the field. He didn't believe any of the accusations against the Dr. Harmon and started making plans to get revenge against Hugo and the other seven alleged victims. To Lapin these eight were just agents of the Devil who were, no doubt, just paving the way for the Beast to bring about the Anti-Christ and his one world government. And, of course, agents of the Devil deserved no mercy.

18

Girl Of His Dreams

Joe got his arm out of the cast right after *The Late Great Hour* was canceled. His left arm was white and slightly atrophied from lack of use. None of his plans to quit his job or move to Yucca Valley had moved forward at all. He called Steve one night to talk but Steve was busy and said he'd call back. He didn't call back for over a week. Joe missed it when he did call back and heard the short three second message later, "Hey dude, Steve here. Later".

On Sunday, dressed in his Sunday casuals, including his favorite sleeveless Springsteen T-shirt, Joe headed to Ralphs, not just to shop but to see if there might be any job openings. He figured he could at least get a job application. The store was crowded as usual but Joe was able to talk to the manager.

"No jobs at the moment," the manager said looking at Joe and his Sunday casual outfit from head to toe, "but check back in a few weeks." Joe decided he'd dress differently next time he checked about a job.

Joe took his groceries home, pumped up the tires of his beach cruiser, and decided to take a nice Sunday bike ride down by the beach. Vaping large clouds of smoke, Joe pedaled off down the street towards the beach bike path. He hoped he wouldn't run into Ricky and Suze or any of the bike crew from the Thursday night happy hour. It had been weeks since Joe had last seen any of the crew and not one person had called, emailed, or messaged to wonder where he had been. Joe figured he hadn't been missed very much.

The bike path was full of bike riders and roller-bladers. Joe rode along at a casual pace towards the Belmont Pier. As he neared Temple Avenue, he thought he saw Ricky and Suze with a few other bike riders in the distance, up the path. *Crap*, thought Joe and he stopped his bike, turned around and quickly started back the other direction. At Junipero Avenue he left the beach bike path and headed up towards Broadway. He took a right at Second Street, just before he got to Broadway, to bike through the residential neighborhood with lots of beautiful, expensive homes. He was headed to Gallagher's for a burger and a cold beer. He didn't miss the Thursday night crew that much but he missed the food at Gallagher's.

The pub was full of people on this Sunday afternoon and an Irish band was playing. Joe found a place at the bar and ordered a pint. In moments he had a nice cold Stone IPA sitting in front of him and a burger ordered. He cheered to no one in particular and took his first sip – so refreshing after a bike ride. He sat on his barstool and observed the people in the bar. He noticed a couple of people from the Thursday night crew were sitting on the far side of the pub. He couldn't remember their names and they hadn't noticed him. Sitting with the Thursday night people was a beautiful blonde girl who looked a lot like the girl of his dreams. Trying not to be noticed he watched the group of people, especially the girl. Her eyes sparkled when she talked.

After a while his burger arrived and he focused on the food. When he had finished his burger he looked around and the girl wasn't at the table anymore. He secretly kept a watch for her but she didn't return. After a short bit, the rest of the people at the table paid their bill and left. It was late in the afternoon and the Irish band finished their set and started to pack up their gear. Joe finished his beer, paid his bill and left. As he rode down Broadway towards home he decided that maybe he'd go to the Thursday night Happy Hour again, just in case the girl he had seen might show up.

On Thursday evening Joe got home from work, quickly shaved, showered, and put on his classic Born To Run t-shirt. He jumped in his car and drove across town to Gallagher's. As he walked through the door he looked for the blonde girl but she wasn't there. He saw Ricky and Suze with just a couple other people. It was still early and certainly more people would arrive soon.

Joe shook hands with Ricky. Suze gave him a friendly hug. Sitting at the table was Clifford, the cross-country traveler, Annie who had escaped from Oakland, Dave, a guitarist, and Dave's girlfriend Ella. Everyone greeted Joe warmly and asked where he had been. Joe told them about his trip to Joshua Tree and Yucca Valley, he elaborated on the story to give the impression he had been out in the desert for the last month. Dave and Ella talked for a while about wanting to move to Joshua Tree. Ricky laughed at the idea and said, "who would want to live in such place?" Suze joined in with a short cheer for Long Beach. Dave pretended to throw a couple of punches at Ricky. Soon a few more people arrived and then a few more, but still no blonde girl.

Joe was into his second beer and a conversation with Annie

about Bruce Springsteen, the first time anyone in the group had shown any interest in talking about the Boss, when Cindi walked in with her date, Gary. Gary was tall, and handsome in a movie star kind of way.

"I recognize you," said Cindi when she was introduced to Joe.

"What?" Joe was confused and the music in the pub was loud.

"I recognize you from a photo my mom sent me, your name is Joe, right?" asked Cindi. Joe had a puzzled look on his face as Cindi got out her phone. After she sat down she scrolled through her text messages until she found what she was looking for. She handed her phone across the table to Joe who took it and saw a photo of himself standing with Mike Wilson. Leslie had taken the photo during their barbecue several weeks ago. It was the first time Joe had seen the picture. Joe handed the phone back to Cindi and introduced himself. Cindi introduced herself, again, and then introduced Gary to Joe.

Joe didn't like Gary right off the bat, and for more than the obvious reason – it was the fake plastic smile Gary gave Joe when they shook hands that really bothered him. Joe had this guy all figured out in the first minute. He had met people like Gary before and they weren't his kind of people. Then Gary pointed at Joe's T-shirt. "Tramps like us man," he said. It sounded blasphemous when Gary quoted the Boss. Now Joe really knew he didn't care for this guy.

19

Want To Bet?

Jeremiah had been wondering for weeks if this street preaching routine was going to last all the way up until the final day. He was really tired of it but kept going because the Almighty hadn't told him to stop. Jeremiah had been beaten-up by a group of punk kids since the last time we checked in with him. Sure, he could have called down fire from heaven to burn his attackers to a crisp, but the attack wasn't that bad. He would have called down fire if the situation had turned truly dangerous. Without a doubt the last few weeks had been tough, but today was different.

Today there were 282 days left to go until the end of the world and Jeremiah had a little bounce in his step. Maybe it was the late summer weather or maybe it was that he could see the end approaching now that it was less than a year away. Maybe it was the astrological calm before the storm or maybe it was the really delicious breakfast burrito he had at the taqueria on Fourth Street. Whatever the reason, Jeremiah began to feel like he had turned a corner of some kind.

Jeremiah spent the morning in the park near the lagoon by the golf course. His audience was the mothers and fathers watching their children in the playground at the lagoon. His audience didn't stick around very long. Nothing cleared a park like an end-times preacher. New groups of parents would show up, hear Jeremiah preaching from his prophet cart with the sign on the side stating 282 days until the end of the world, then quickly leave.

The police showed up around 1:30 and escorted Jeremiah out of the park. The officers were familiar with Jeremiah, having responded to complaints about the street preacher a number of times in the last few years. During the two mile long walk home from the lagoon, as Jeremiah dragged his prophet cart behind him, he sensed today was an important day.

When Jeremiah reached the corner of Broadway and Redondo Avenue he wheeled his prophet cart into the bar called The Reno Room.

"No preaching in the bar," called out the bartender when he saw Jeremiah with his cart.

"Don't worry Johnny Mac, no more preaching today. How about a cold one?"

Johnny poured Jeremiah his usual Stone IPA and placed it in front of him on the bar.

"None of that turning water into beer today, okay?" Johnny winked at Jeremiah referring to the small miracle Jeremiah had performed a year earlier.

Jeremiah pulled a ten out of his wallet and laid it on the bar. "Keep the change," he said.

Jeremiah sipped his beer and kept his eye on the front door. His intuition, or maybe it was the Holy Spirit, told him someone important was going to walk through the door shortly. For a half hour a few people came and went but no one stood out to Jeremiah. Then a girl walked in, and the way the light shone behind her – it was like a vision. He knew this was the person, she was so beautiful.

Karen James was actually a rather plain girl, but that's not the way she appeared to Jeremiah. To him she looked like an angel, a dream come true. Karen had come into the bar for some reason, which escaped her the minute the bar door closed. It had been a hectic and scattered day. It was like the wind was blowing her to and fro. The only chair available at the bar was next to Jeremiah, so Karen settled in and ordered a Stone IPA.

Karen checked her make-up as she waited for her beer. She smiled nervously at the handsome older guy sitting next to her. The couple on the other side of her completely ignored her. Karen focused on the baseball game on the TV over the bar.

"The Dodgers are going to win this one," Jeremiah spoke up, trying to break the ice.

"Huh?" replied Karen, not expecting Jeremiah to speak to her.

"Dodgers," he pointed at the TV set, "they're going to win this one." The Dodgers were down by five runs and it was half way through the sixth inning.

"No way, the Yankees' got this one nearly wrapped up."

"Want to bet?" asked Jeremiah, this was going to be an easy win, "I'll bet you a cigarette."

"You're on," replied Karen and she reached over and shook Jeremiah's hand.

The two watched the rest of the game together, each cheering for their respective teams. The Dodgers mounted a stunning comeback and won the game by one run.

Karen looked over at Jeremiah suspiciously. "How did you know that the Dodgers would win?"

Jeremiah smiled, "How about we go have a cigarette and I'll tell you."

"Back in a minute, Johnny," he said to the bartender. Johnny Mac nodded and smiled. *The preacher has a girl*, he thought.

Jeremiah had learned long ago to be honest with the ladies about his calling as a prophet, it headed off troubles down the road. Of course, he hadn't yet met one woman who was interested in him once they found out about his whole end-of-the-world preaching gig. But still he was sure honesty was the best policy.

Karen was fascinated by Jeremiah and his calling as a prophet. More than fascinated. This was actually what she was looking for in a man: good solid beliefs in God, spirituality, and a prophet to boot. Karen's father had been a deeply religious man and it had made a strong impression on her growing up. Now, without really knowing it, she was looking for a man like her father, a devout and principled man.

One cigarette turned into two and then several more beers. Jeremiah told Karen all about his mission and that there were only 282 more days left before the end of the world. Karen was happy to hear the news, she thought the world was already past its due date. It was sometime after seven when the two left the Reno Room. Jeremiah walked Karen to her car and they exchanged phone numbers. Jeremiah watched Karen drive away and said a little prayer about her getting home safely. He wasn't quite sure about it, but he thought he might be in love.

Jeremiah walked home, dragging his prophet cart behind him. He thought about his arrangement with The Man Upstairs. For the last twenty-five years God had prepared him for his current project. Everything that came into his life had to do with the future, the end of days. Like a tough sports coach, God had hardened him to do what needed to be done. The Almighty had put the whole responsibility for the operation into Jeremiah's hands. It was Jeremiah's call if God should pull the plug on the planet. As Jeremiah understood it, God would be waiting for his word on May 25th. It would be a prayer from Jeremiah that would set in motion the events that would end life as we know it on planet Earth.

A person might wonder why God would do things in such a way. That is, after all, a lot of responsibility to put on one person's shoulders. And I agree, but this was God's way of doing things. He spent years looking for the right person for this job and his search had led Him to Jeremiah. After years of training Jeremiah was prepared and ready to do what he needed, which was essentially killing over seven billion people. God hadn't even guaranteed his survival, so in Jeremiah's mind this was a suicide mission. If he went through with it. Now, pulling his cart home with love on his mind he was having the first doubts about the mission he'd had in a long time.

20

Cindi's Move

It had been a particularly bad Tuesday at work. Bill Diamond, Joe's boss, was trying to get rid of all the Latino workers. This week, so far, he had fired three of the best crew members Joe had had in a long time, including Roberto and Xavier. All the reasons for the firings had been ridiculous, but that didn't seem to matter. Bill was on a mission, in spite of the harm it was doing the company. So far no one acceptable to Bill had responded to the help wanted ads and Joe was down three hard workers with the same amount of work to accomplish.

After work Joe found his car had a flat tire. One of his workers helped him change his tire and Joe gave him twenty bucks. That worker was fired by Bill the next day. The ride home from Wilmington took longer than usual due to several accidents. And it was hot – sticky, rather humid and hot. Joe's air conditioning in his old Honda Civic was starting to die and only worked sporadically on the ride home.

When he got home his door step was wet. It smelled like someone had pissed on his porch. After he had hosed off his front porch he grabbed a cold beer and went out back. He slammed the back door closed and scared the neighborhood cat hanging out in the backyard. He was in a bad mood, pissed at the world. He vaped, drank and stewed about what a crappy day it had been. The first beer turned into a second and then a third. Then Joe's phone rang, but he didn't recognized the number and let it go to the message.

"Hi Joe," it was Cindi's voice on the message, "this is Cindi. I got your number from my mom, I hope you don't mind. I'm going to Joshua Tree this weekend to see my folks and I was wondering if, you, ah, wanted to come along... roooad trip!" When Cindi said road trip she sounded like a cheerleader. "Anyway, call me back or I'll see you on Thursday, bye." Joe was in shock. He listened to the message several times, just to hear the sound of Cindi's voice. He wondered about Gary. Cindi hadn't mentioned Gary, would he be coming along too? Her message sure didn't sound like it but Joe didn't want to get his hopes up, it hadn't exactly been a good day and another disappointment or setback wasn't welcome.

Joe got a fresh beer to sip on and called Cindi back. Once the phone started ringing he realized how buzzed he was and hung up. His phone rang almost immediately. He could see it was Cindi calling.

"This is Joe," said Joe, answering the call.

"Hi Joe, this is Cindi," came a cheerful voice from the other end of the line.

"Joshua Tree! Road trip," blurted out Joe, trying not to sound too buzzed.

"Yeah, I'm going up there this weekend to see my parents. I thought you might want to get away for a day trip." Cindi's voice sounded tempting. But what about Gary?

"Who all is going?" asked Joe.

"Oh, just me. It's a long drive and I hate to do the drive by myself. Plus you know my folks already and they like you."

"Isn't Gary coming?" Joe just had to make sure.

"Oh boy, Gary," there was laughter in Cindi's voice, "no, Gary won't be able to make it. Business or something. Really, I just met him a few weeks ago and it's not like he's my boyfriend or anything."

"Oh, okay," Joe started to reply but Cindi cut him off,

"I mean, this isn't a date, it's just a road trip."

Joe could feel Cindi's face turning red on the other end of the line.

"No, I didn't think of it like that," replied Joe who wished that it was a date.

"So, have you ever seen Bruce live?" asked Cindi, changing the subject. Suze had told her Joe was a big Springsteen fan, "He's amazing." Cindi had seen Bruce once.

"I've seen him four times," replied Joe and with that a twenty minute conversation about the Boss was launched. That led to another half hour of conversation about the day Joe had, life, family and Cindi's work at Ralphs before the two hung up.

When Cindi hung up the phone she told herself to not get too excited, then she called her mom.

"Hi Mom, what's up, and, ahhhhh, what are you and Dad doing this weekend?" started Cindi.

"Why nothing Cindi, why do you ask?" questioned her mom.

"I wanted to come visit, and I'm going to bring a friend with me, Joe Smith," replied Cindi and she told her mom about the plans she had in mind. Leslie was thrilled that they were going to see Joe again.

That Thursday Joe and Cindi sat next to each other at Happy Hour and discussed their plans for the upcoming weekend. The rest of the bike crew was planning a bike ride for that weekend and everyone pretty much left Joe and Cindi alone while they talked. Suze wasn't the only one that noticed how cozy the two were becoming as they leaned towards each other, engrossed in conversation.

Gary showed up later and said, "What's up boss?" to Joe before he grabbed a chair from another table and squeezed between Joe and Cindi. Ten minutes later Gary and Cindi said good night to everyone and left. Joe had just ordered a fresh beer, so he stayed around talking with Suze and Clifford while mentally preoccupied with Cindi – and Gary. He really did not like this Gary character, his smile was cheap and he acted like he owned Cindi. At least this weekend Gary wouldn't be around.

21

Roooad Trip!

Cindi picked Joe up on Saturday morning around 9:00 wearing a flowered sundress and sandals. She was driving because Joe's car wasn't in any shape to make the Joshua Tree trip in the late summer with its air conditioning dying. Cindi had a much newer car, a red Toyota truck with great air conditioning.

Joe was ready to go when Cindi arrived, wearing his U2 *Joshua Tree* t-shirt and Miami shorts. He quickly showed her around his apartment before grabbing his cooler and putting it in the back of her truck. Cindi liked Joe's place. He had actual paintings on the wall instead of posters or blank walls. She was impressed with the size of his record collection, especially his Bruce and U2 albums. She could see that they were going to have no problem listening to music together.

"You can vape in my truck, I don't mind," said Cindi.

Joe had been standing outside the truck, vaping a few hits before getting on the road, "Really? Thanks," and Joe hopped into her truck. The interior was clean with a small dream catcher hanging from rear view mirror. Cindi had a binder of CDs which Joe started to peruse as Cindi began to navigate the way out of Long Beach towards the freeway. She had nearly as many U2 albums as he did, along with every Bruce album. There was a big selection of eighties music along with some classic rock. Joe felt at home looking through her CDs.

"See anything you want to hear?" asked Cindi.

"How about some Rolling Stones to start the drive?" asked Joe, holding up the *Exile On Main Street* CD. He took a vape hit and blew it out the window. "Driving to the desert makes me want to hear the Rolling Stones for some reason."

"Excellent choice," said Cindi smiling.

The miles started to roll out under them as they moved from one freeway to another, and soon they were through Orange County and headed towards Riverside. The conversation drifted casually as they talked about movies, bikes, music and books. As well as they connected over music they were different about their tastes in movies and books. Cindi liked fantasy novels, romantic comedies and costume dramas. Joe liked action and horror movies, American literature like John Steinbeck and really disliked costume dramas.

"So what's up with Gary?" Joe asked after they had been on the road an hour. Joe was nervous asking about Gary, afraid of the answer.

"I met him at work a few weeks ago, I helped him find something on the shelves and he asked me out." Cindi stared at the road as she answered. She knew this question had been coming and wasn't looking forward to answering it.

"Just like that?"

"Well, he came in the store a few times, and we had talked some before he asked me out."

"Are you still going out?" Joe didn't really want to know the answer but he asked anyways.

"No. Well, kind of yes, but not really,"

Cindi glanced over at Joe. He had a puzzled look on his face.

"I mean, he keeps calling me. But he's kind of strange and I don't think I want to go out with him again. He's gotten really possessive, quickly, and that reminds me of Shane." She glanced again at Joe and could see he was still confused. "Shane is my ex-fiancee."

"Ex-fiancee? How long ago was that?"

"We broke up earlier this year. We went out for three years. Shane cheated on me before the wedding and I called it off."

"My ex-fiancee cheated on me too. I found out two weeks before we were going to get married. She screwed my best friend at the time. Really messed me up."

"Me too. I was a wreck. It's why I left Bakersfield and moved to Long Beach," Cindi looked over at Joe. She was really starting to like the look of his face, especially now that he was transforming from an acquaintance into a friend. She spent the next ten minutes telling Joe all about her break-up with Shane.

"Well, fuck Shane," said Joe when she was done, and Cindi laughed, "Yeah, fuuuuuck Shane!" Again she sounded like a cheerleader when she said it.

The Rolling Stones CD came to an end and started to repeat, neither of them noticed as they continued talking. Soon they left the freeway for the highway, Highway 62, and after another forty-five minutes they were pulling into Joshua Tree. Cindi drove to a parking lot near the laundromat to call her parents and let them know they'd be there shortly.

22

Ancient Biological Activities

Mike watched his daughter pull up in her truck with Joe in the passenger seat. *Joe!* He was so glad that Cindi hadn't brought Gary. On the phone one evening Cindi had described Gary to him and it had made him want to scream. He sounded like another Shane. Joe was a different story. He was glad to see him again. *Maybe, for once, Cindi will make a good choice in men,* he thought. Leslie was thinking pretty much the same thing as she looked out the front window and saw Cindi's truck pull up with Joe riding shotgun.

Mike had been waiting until his daughter arrived to smoke his first joint of the day. He knew a joint would be just what she needed after the two and a half hour drive from Long Beach. Mike had just got a quarter ounce of a strain called JK Special from his dealer and had rolled a large joint from his stash to share with his daughter. His dealer said the pot was grown by a wizard in the San Bernardino Mountains. Mike, who wasn't sure if he believed his dealer, was still working on the art of rolling joints, so the joint wasn't exactly perfect, but it served it purpose. Soon after the two had arrived Mike lit up the fatty and passed it around. Cindi inhaled several large hits off the joint while Joe took a few little hits, trying not to get too stoned.

The JK Special turned out to be really special and soon Cindi had gotten out her parents photo scrapbooks and memories and stories were being shared. Leslie made sandwiches – beers, wine and iced tea were served – and the afternoon segued into the evening and a barbecue in the backyard. The sun set, the stars came out and Mike lit a blazing fire in the fire pit.

Another fat joint was smoked while everyone enjoyed the glow of the fire. Joe was sitting next to Cindi, and as he looked over at her he couldn't resist, he leaned over and planted a small kiss on her cheek. Cindi turned towards him, smiled, reached over and gently held the sides of his face. She placed a kiss on his lips and Joe kissed her back. Neither cared that Cindi's parents were right there. Mike looked over at Leslie and they smiled at each other. Mike gave a small, discreet thumbs-up in Leslie's direction.

It was getting late as the fire started to wane. Many beers and glasses of wine had been consumed by this point. Mike insisted that Cindi and Joe spend the night and drive back to Long Beach the next day. It was decided that Cindi would stay in the guest room and Joe would sleep on the sofa in the living room.

Later that night, when the house had gotten quiet, Cindi came into the living room and woke Joe. She led him back to her room and the two made love. The two were comfortable with each other like two puzzle pieces finally finding each other. Cindi lay in the bed holding on to Joe for a while before he got up to go back to the sofa. As he got up he kissed her and told her he loved her. "Me too," said Cindi, sleepily.

Joe laid awake on the sofa for a long while before falling asleep. He thought about Cindi, of course. He was in love. He knew it and everything was different than it had been just a day earlier. He not only liked, he *loved* this family, Cindi and her parents. He had no idea how all this was going to play out in the days ahead but for now he had a hope for the future he hadn't felt in a long time, maybe since he was a kid.

Cindi fell asleep right away. She knew the future was going to be just fine. She was so content. The guest room smelled like her parents house usually smelled, no matter how many times they moved, and it always made her feel at peace. And then there was Joe. She had never met a guy quite like Joe. Joe treated her kindly and with respect. That was something she could definitely get used to. As she drifted off to sleep, deep inside her, ancient biological activities were at work. One of Joe's sperm reached Cindi's egg, and did what sperm and egg have been doing for millions of years. The fertilized egg soon split into two cells, then four, then eight and a new life began.

Mike, attuned to the sounds of the house, heard the door of Cindi's room open late at night. He heard it close again and the muffled sounds from the room next door. Later he woke when he heard Cindi's door open and close again. He heard Joe moving around in the living room and then the house was quiet once more.

Leslie slept through the night, but she had the strangest dream about traveling through space. Mike, Cindi and Joe were all in her dream, and there was a child, a special child with unusual gifts – her grandchild. The dream lasted for what seemed to be years until the ship they were traveling on arrived at a far distant planet. Approaching its destination the ship went out of control and was crashing into the planet when she suddenly woke up. The morning light was cold and the sudden ending of her dream with flames, explosions and death had unsettled her. Leslie lay in bed for the next hour as the sun rose and the sounds of the morning birds – the quails, the scrub jays and the doves – filtered into the room.

23

Joe's Breakfast Special

Joe woke before everyone else and walked around outside, vaping and enjoying the view of the Morongo Basin and Joshua Tree National Park from Mike and Leslie's house. There was a slight breeze that was crisp and dry. While he was looking at the cholla-filled lot across the street he saw a coyote run by. He saw a snake but it wasn't a rattler, and it quickly disappeared into the underbrush. He watched a roadrunner catch a lizard.

When he got back to the house Mike was up and putting on coffee. Leslie was making herself busy in the kitchen. Joe asked if he could prepare breakfast for everyone. He had already inspected the refrigerator and pantry – everything he needed to whip up a Joe's Breakfast Special was available. Joe's Breakfast Special was a Heuvos Rancheros extravaganza with bacon, eggs, rice, refried beans, guacamole, caramelized onions, tortillas, salsa and sour cream. When Cindi finally woke up and wandered into the kitchen Joe gave her a kiss and got started cooking up his extravaganza. Mike winked at Leslie when he saw Joe kiss Cindi. *Love seems to be blossoming*, Mike thought.

The breakfast was a success, but Cindi seemed preoccupied. Shortly after breakfast was done she said she needed to get back to Long Beach and they needed to leave soon. Joe, who was still getting to know Cindi wasn't sure what to make of her strange mood, went with it and said he had to get back to Long Beach too. Mike was busy rolling up a joint and tried not to let his disappointment show. He had been looking forward to hanging out all day with Joe and Cindi. By 11:30 the two were back on the road, headed back to Long Beach. Mike and Leslie stood in the driveway and watched them drive off, waving as Cindi's truck disappeared from sight.

The drive back to Long Beach was filled with long silences and occasional small talk – Cindi seemed to be in a really tense mood. Halfway home she seemed to loosen up and relax but Joe wondered where the closeness he had felt lying next to her last night had gone. Cindi dropped Joe and his cooler off and didn't even get out of the truck when she pulled up at his apartment. She gave him a quick hug and a kiss through the window before driving off. Joe stood in front of his apartment holding his cooler, watching her drive away, perplexed.

Cindi had felt out of sorts that morning and a bit hungover – that was more wine than she was used to drinking. Then she remembered making love with Joe. Even though it had seemed like a good idea at the time she wondered if that had been a mistake. First off, she still had Gary trying to date her, and now Joe said he was in love with her. She sure liked Joe, a lot, but love… she wasn't ready for these complications in her life. The whole thing had given her a headache. She was barely making sense of life since her break up with Shane and move from Bakersfield. She wished the world would just stop for a while so she could get her bearings.

But the world wasn't going to stop and she had things to take care of before work the next day: clothes to wash, shopping to do, phone calls to return. Gary had left several messages on her voicemail, and he sounded upset. Joe slipped to the back of her mind as she rolled up a joint and smoked it before getting to work on her chores.

24

Tsunami

Lately there had been no peace of mind for Jeremiah. His days were filled with preaching his end-times message in parks and street corners around Long Beach, dragging his prophet cart behind him. People had no qualms about throwing insults at him while he preached. His only relief from the terrors he beheld for the planet was the kernel of love growing in his heart for Karen James. It was 272 days until the end of the world.

That night, when Jeremiah slept he had a troubling dream. He was on a beach, trying to get people's attention but no one would listen to him. People told him to shut up and people told him to go away. Jeremiah was watching the water recede from the shoreline. He knew what came next, a tsunami. The water receded further and further from the shore as many people, full of curiosity, went down onto the newly revealed beach. The water just kept receding. Somewhere out near the horizon a bulge was growing in the ocean. A powerful wave was rapidly racing towards the shore.

Jeremiah felt himself straining to yell in his dream, screaming at the people on the beach, but no one moved to leave. Jeremiah turned to run from the shore but the beach started to curve upwards at impossible angles. Jeremiah ran and ran through the soft sand getting nowhere. He seemed to be the only one seeing the giant tsunami coming. Jeremiah turned to face the tsunami, put out one hand and commanded the wave, "STOP!", and the wave froze in place and then collapsed harmlessly back into the ocean. Slowly and peacefully the water began to refill the area it had receded from moments earlier. The people exploring the new beach retreated safely and soon all was back to normal.

Jeremiah figured his dream was about the coming end of the world. Was the dream a message from The Almighty? Even after twenty-five years on this prophet job, there were always strange, nuanced messages from The Man Upstairs that needed to be interpreted. The Almighty is not only long-winded but is a bit of a poet and artist too. Was God trying to tell him not to end the world after all, or was He telling him that he wouldn't be able to go through with it? Or was there a different, more subtle message? Or was this just indigestion from the pizza he ate before bed?

Jeremiah laid awake for an hour thinking about the tsunami and the coming end of the world. After a while he got up and put on a Bob Dylan album. Bob Dylan was his go-to musician when he had things to figure out. He put on the album *Slow Train Coming* and sat in his big chair contemplating, as he had so many times before, what the end would be like. Fire from heaven was his preference, a massive meteor attack or asteroid impact, or something like that, but definitely fire. This time the cycle of the ages would come to an end with fire.

While it was still dark outside Jeremiah got dressed and ate a piece of toast. He slipped out the front door of his apartment and headed to the beach. The first light of dawn was beginning to show as Jeremiah reached the bluff above the beach. The sun coming up lit the sky on fire with color. Hardly anyone was around except for early morning joggers. Jeremiah walked towards the water and spent the next twenty minutes doing his Tai Chi exercises.

Feeling full of energy, Jeremiah bowed down towards the rising sun and began his morning prayers. He prayed for Long Beach, for California and the United States. He prayed for the world and all the creatures that live upon it. He prayed blessings on the fault lines to prevent any earthquakes. He prayed for the weather. Today he prayed for rain. In spite of weather reports saying this was going to be a clear day, the sky slowly darkened and by the time Jeremiah was walking home a half hour later a gentle rain was falling on Long Beach. Long Beach, I'd like to note, looks especially appealing when it rains.

Jeremiah got back home and put on some coffee. Even a street preacher needs to take a day off every so often and today was going to be one of those days for Jeremiah. He was just going to let the gentle rain fall all day. He had a lot on his mind, the dream the night before had given him pause to reconsider the future of the world. He thought he'd call Karen later and see what she was doing on this rainy day.

As you might have guessed, Jeremiah had a certain amount of control over the weather. Weather, earthquakes, volcanoes, climate changes – control over all these things had been given into Jeremiah's hands by the Almighty. This was, of course, an insane amount of responsibility to put into anyone's hands, but like I mentioned before, the Almighty had handpicked Jeremiah for this job. This had been training for the ultimate responsibility of deciding on the fate of the seven billion individuals on the planet.

But now, Karen had entered the picture, which confused the issue further. Jeremiah suspected that The Man Upstairs was behind Karen showing up in his life. God often had a way of playing both sides of an issue to force humans to make decisions. Complications, Jeremiah had learned, were often God's way of moving his thinking to the next level. As I've mentioned before, God was as tough on his best players as any sports coach would be.

25

Revenge

While collecting fossils under his alias as Samuel Livingston, Jacques Lapin was plotting to bring down Hugo Von Schmidt, Dr. Harmon's assailant. He had gathered a massive amount of information about Hugo and the other seven men who had come out against Dr. Charles Harmon.

Dr. Harmon had recovered from his gunshot wound but not from the accusations of molestation. David Monroe, one of the seven men, had initiated a civil lawsuit against the doctor. Using social media, David launched a campaign against pedophilia in the Protestant church. In the first few weeks of the campaign more than a dozen men and women had come out about their childhood experiences and several prominent evangelical preacher's careers came to an abrupt end as more lawsuits were filed.

David Monroe was blown up by a mailbomb a month after the social media campaign started. Jacques Lapin had mailed the bomb. It was his first analog terrorist attack in ages and he felt pretty good about it. One down, seven to go.

Hugo Von Schmidt, who was out on bail, was arrested a week later for child pornography on his computer. Lapin was responsible for planting the porn on Hugo's computer using a sophisticated computer attack. Lapin had also tipped the authorities off about Von Schmidt. Two down...

Soon there were internet attacks leading to financial ruin and false arrest warrants issued. Several more mailbombings took place. The eight men who had come out against Dr. Harmon had all been dealt with in one way or another by Jacques Lapin. The social media campaign fizzled out after the bombings and the FBI had few leads on the attacks, which were all apparently connected or coordinated by the same people. Meanwhile, in Utah, Samuel Livingston was working on and off with a *National Geographic* television crew, digging up dinosaur bones. Jacques Lapin, as usual, had an airtight alibi, if the need ever came up in the future.

FBI agent Jim Dalton was in charge of the case of the mailbombings. As a twenty-two year veteran of the Bureau, Dalton remembered Jacques Lapin, his first case has been a bank bombing in the late 1990s. Lapin's trail had gone cold years earlier but Dalton had a good memory. Something about the few remains from the mailbombs reminded him of the bank bombings years earlier. Similar to the series of bank bombings, no one had stepped forward and taken credit for the attacks. Dalton's old supervisor had compiled a large file on Lapin before the trail went cold and now Dalton went back to the filling cabinets and retrieved the old file. Here is a bit of what the file said:

Jacques Lapin was born in Quebec, Canada. His working class parents had both been Christian anarchist revolutionaries and raised Jacques for a life of subversive revolution. The father, Emile Lapin, had taught young Jacques to build bombs by the time he was nine. His mother, Yvonne Lapin, taught young Jacques the fine art of poisoning. Together they trained him in hand-to-hand combat, armed warfare, and wiretapping, toughening him to be an ever-ready solider in the eternal, and world-wide, battle against evil – against the inevitable rise of the Anti-Christ.

Lapin's previous obsessions with the end-times was commented on several places in the extensive notes in the file. Dalton made a mental note about it because the mailbombings all had a connection to Dr. Harmon. He decided to drive up to Cincinnati to visit Dr. Harmon and see if there was anything he could learn.

26

The Silence Of Heaven

Charles Harmon had just gotten off the phone with his lawyer, who was very busy these days. The doctor's wife of fifty-four years, Mary, was in the process of divorcing him. The revelations about the decades old molestations and the social media campaign had caused irreparable damage to his reputation. Charles remembered every one of the men who had come out against him. He knew these weren't the only ones, there were others who had kept quiet so far. He didn't know how long that would last.

Charles was exhausted from the events of the last couple months. The gunshot to his gut had missed everything vital and the wound was still in the process of healing. He had spent a week in the hospital recovering and just hadn't felt right, physically, since the shooting. Morally and spiritually he felt dead. Von Schmidt had successfully killed a part of him, but it was a part of him that had been wounded for a long time. Lately, for the first time in decades, Charles had spent time on his knees in prayer. No one seemed to have any interest or use for him anymore, he wondered if God did.

"Dear Heavenly Father," began Charles, kneeling by his bed that night, "I have fallen short. Oh, Lord I've failed miserably. I've ruined everything you've given me. I've ruined lives and now

Mary has left me. Take my life Lord, take my life..." and he broke down sobbing, his hands clutched together fiercely, rocking and quivering on his knees.

Heaven was quiet and did not answer Charles.

27

Me Too, She Said

Joe called in sick to work on Monday after the road trip. He had new plans again, and these new plans had to do with finally getting a new job. The weekend with Cindi had given him the sense of motivation he had been lacking. He wanted something better, and now that things seemed to be moving the right direction, he did his best to grab a hold of the momentum and let it pull him along. He dressed up in his only suit and decided to tackle the several different grocery stores in town: Ralphs, Vons, and Stater Brothers.

Surprisingly, after filling out applications at several stores, Joe was interviewed and hired as a stock clerk at Vons. He called Cindi with the good news, but got her voicemail. He told her he was going to Gallagher's to celebrate and that she should come by if she got his message in time, he planned on being there a while.

Joe had finished several pints by the time Cindi returned his call. She was so happy for him, but no, she couldn't join him for a drink. She had to get to work. Joe, in his exuberance, told Cindi how she had motivated him to make this career move. Then Joe told Cindi he loved her. She paused a moment and then replied, "me too." Even though Joe was buzzed, the pause wasn't lost on him. His mood dropped a notch and he made an excuse to get off the phone.

Joe sat, looking at his phone and his beer for a while, wondering about Cindi's non-committal sounding "me too". He went and sat outside in the smoking section to vape and drink his next beer. While he sat there the girl at the next table started talking to him. She had dark brown hair and a pretty face. Her name was Tracy and she was waiting for a friend to arrive. While they chatted Joe told her about his new job.

Tracy tipped her glass towards Joe. "That's a cause for celebration, cheers," she said. Joe cheered her and took a long drink. The two continued to talk and it wasn't long before Joe learned that Tracy was quite a Bruce Springsteen fan. She had seen Bruce twice, once she was even pulled up on stage to dance with the Boss. Joe was impressed and it seemed like some kind of synchronicity when *Dancing In The Dark* started playing on the jukebox right after she told him that.

Tracy's friend Cheryl showed up a little bit later and Tracy asked Joe if he'd join them for dinner. Joe, now drinking his fourth beer, thought that sounded like a great idea and excused himself to go to the bathroom. Tracy quickly gave Cheryl the lowdown while Joe was gone.

"I saw him first," said Tracy with a smile.

"Maybe I'll share him with you," replied Cheryl, twisting her long blonde hair with her finger. She adjusted her low-cut top just a bit to make sure her cleavage was more prominent. Tracy laughed. It wouldn't be the first time they had shared a guy.

"No, I mean it this time, I saw him first," Tracy gave Cheryl a more serious look.

Joe returned to the table like a fly walking into a spider web.

28

Special Agent
Sam Eastwind

On September 7th there were 260 day left until the end of the world. Claude's dreams had been changing for the last couple of weeks and he was making note of it. The end-of-the-world dreams had been dwindling and instead he had numerous dreams where nothing happened but regular stuff like going shopping, people gathered at a festival in a park, barbecues, and people driving on highways. There was one night where he had a disturbing dream about a tsunami with a crazy man running around on a beach, but the crazy man had stopped the tsunami with a word. Claude reported all these dreams to Aristotle. Because he was being so well paid by the psychic, he had quit his job at the pizza joint and now spent his days in a leisurely fashion with plenty of time for dreaming. He wondered if this leisure time was having an effect on his dreams.

Then the spaceship dreams started. They came regularly, night after night for a week. Simple dreams really, rather ordinary glimpses into the life of humans aboard spaceships in a giant fleet crossing the vast reaches of the cosmos. The spaceships were headed to Earth, Claude knew it from overhearing various crew members talking, but they were still light-years away. The best

Claude could gather was that the fleet would arrive early the next year.

Aristotle was deeply interested in these latest dreams. Several of his staff psychics had reported spaceship visions the previous week. A couple of his psychics had dreams and visions about some terrorist-like event that involved many spaceships and flying marbles. Aristotle compiled the latest dream reports and emailed them off to the First Lady's secretary.

Due to Aristotle's contacts with the White House, the CIA, who routinely intercepted email going to the White House, had become interested in his reports to the First Lady and consequentially May 25th. Special Agent Sam Eastwind was put on the case with instructions to report to the director of the agency. Sam immediately booked a flight to California. He was going to make an appointment with this psychic and get to the bottom of the issue. After years on the job Sam had learned the valuable lesson that the solution to every case was found by getting to the bottom of the issue.

Hours later Sam was checked into his room at the Motel 6 in West Hollywood. As usual, Sam was keeping this trip low key, he was undercover. His cover story for this trip was that he was Vincent Pagoda, a struggling actor from the East Coast, trying to get a start in the movie business. It was an easy story to believe because it was shared by thousands of men and women in Hollywood.

Sam/Vincent had an appointment with Aristotle on Tuesday morning. He mentally prepared himself to meet the renowned psychic. He had been trained by the agency to not only go undercover physically but psychically too. Sam had been chosen for this case because of his above-average psychic abilities. When he went to his appointment he believed he was Vincent Pagoda, stage actor and hopefully soon-to-be-movie-star.

When Sam arrived at Aristotle's psychic shop on Sunset Boulevard, Maria Montello led him into the outer waiting room with the neon fortune teller sign humming over the door to the inner sanctum. After a few minutes the door opened and a voice from inside the room said "Enter." Aristotle was seated in front of his crystal ball at the round table in the center of the darkened room in all his robes and make-up. The goal was to create a theatrical setting that would enhance the psychic reading. The setting worked every time and people tended to believe whatever Aristotle told them.

Sam entered the room and sat at the table across from Aristotle, who seemed to be in a trance with his eyes closed, breathing softly. As Sam sat down Aristotle opened his eyes and peered at Sam like he was looking right through him, which is exactly what Aristotle was doing. The person in front of him was hiding something, he knew it the moment the Special Agent walked in the room. He looked at Sam, letting his psychic senses soak up the reality of the person sitting across from him, and those special senses retrieved all kinds of information from the ether. In moments he had Sam's name and his job and the reason why he was there.

"Good morning, Special Agent Sam Eastwind," said Aristotle after a few minutes.

"No, you're wrong, my name is Vincent Pagoda, I'm an..." started Sam, in protest.

"You're a CIA agent specially trained in psychic warfare. You're thirty-eight years old and recently divorced from Emily, who was your high school sweetheart. You want to know about May 25th and you want to get to the bottom of the issue." Aristotle's stare was penetrating in the way that only a true psychic's can be. He was just warming up, once he called Sam out, more and more details leaked from Sam's mind. Aristotle just kept reading his mail.

Sam quit protesting. He was dealing with a real psychic, not one of the many frauds he had seen in his years at the agency. He closed his mind down, trying to lock down his thoughts. He saw Aristotle smile.

"Where shall I start?" began Aristotle, "Should we talk about how you used to wet your bed, or about the fact that you secretly find men attractive? You know it's nothing to be ashamed of, right?"

Sam could feel his face turning red. He hated psychics and their prying senses. They never played fair.

"Can I be straight with you?" Sam asked.

"Sure. You don't really have any other option," replied Aristotle, who smiled like a Cheshire cat, a Cheshire cat in makeup and robes.

"Okay, I'm after information about May 25th. Can you help me or not?"

"My expertise is information. Of course, everything has a price attached to it."

"We can pay the price, but what kind of information do you have?"

The two talked for another forty-five minutes but Sam didn't learn anything that hadn't been in the intercepted reports to the White House. Aristotle, of course, knew this, and was only too happy to take the agency's money for giving them information they already had.

A little side note about Sam Eastwind, he was a double agent, a fact he kept shielded from Aristotle's psychic prying. His first allegiance was to Black Shield and before he headed back to agency headquarters in Virginia he had already reported his findings to his supervisor at Black Shield. The report about May 25th ended up in front of Nathan Dynasty the next morning.

29

Dun, Dun, Da, Dun

Nathan Dynasty woke up in a terrible mood. His dreams had been awful and he had indigestion from dinner the night before. The sauce on the roast beef had been too rich and it still wasn't agreeing with his system. He sat on his golden toilet and pondered life in all its nastiness.

Life wasn't easy for Nathan these days. His five sons were trying to wrestle control of Black Shield away from him. His wife hadn't slept with him in months, and even though he had more than a few mistresses, it still bothered him. He had gout and irritable bowel syndrome.

He read the report about May 25th while eating a poached egg, his favorite breakfast. The poached egg was runny this morning and he hated that. He called his secretary to have a new breakfast sent in ASAP, and to fire the new chef.

Nathan read Sam's report with interest. He had been busy planning the future of human civilization on planet Earth, which is how he spent his time. Being the richest and most powerful person on the planet, he figured he should have the biggest say on the future of the planet. Every year he would chart out the future with his many advisers and elite associates around the world. Because the future was too valuable to be left in the hands of amateurs, the elite guided its unfolding in a way that benefited them.

The elite met each spring at the Vandenberg Hotel in Bern, Switzerland to secretly discuss their plans for the world for the next year. The Vandenberg Group, as the discussions were known, involved many of the movers and shakers on the planet. At least ninety-five percent of the Vandenberg Group were aliens, or descendants of aliens, from Estes-Sol.

Nathan sat for a while, after eating his second poached egg (which was much better than the first one) and pondered the report about May 25th: Alien spacecraft, a terrorist-like event, a tsunami on the west coast of America, fire and brimstone, meteors and asteroids – the day had many possibilities and none of them were good.

The fateful day was nearly 260 days away, but Nathan wasn't one to put things off. He started making plans right away. He called his top advisers and planned a meeting with his security council that afternoon. That meeting led to a series of meetings and soon people were being mobilized with Nathan's response to the May 25th threats. Deep underground bunkers were prepared, heads of nations were notified, and a number of contingency plans put into motion.

If this book were a major motion picture, right now there would be scenes of action, scenes of military personal moving around purposefully, numerous aircraft taxiing down runways and taking off, serious people talking seriously on phones, and people running around buildings in a determined fashion. Strong, thematic music would be playing with a powerful, anxiety provoking beat. *Dun, dun, da, dun, dun, da, dun...*

30

Worn Out Prophet

Jeremiah and Karen were quickly becoming an item. She would join Jeremiah out in the parks and loved his end-of-the-world speeches. Jeremiah had created handouts that she would pass out to the people who would stop for a second to listen to the street preacher. Karen had become a true believer. Of course she had seen Jeremiah perform his favorite miracle of turning water into beer many times now and knew his gifts were legit.

Lately Jeremiah was having trouble with his end-times sermons. It was as if all his efforts were useless. No one listened, and if they did, what good would it do them? There was no way they could stop the coming destruction and Jeremiah wasn't offering salvation of any kind. But Karen encouraged him to keep it up. So, here he was, once again at the park, standing on his prophet cart, preaching his message of doom while Karen beamed at him with her endearingly goofy smile and large sunglasses.

With less then 230 days to go, he wished the end would be tomorrow so he could be done with this project. He was a worn out prophet with a worn out message and recently The Almighty had gone unusually quiet. If it weren't for the simple miracles Jeremiah performed nearly every day, the multiplying of food, the water into beer, control of the weather, Jeremiah would have ceased to believe in his project.

It was October and the weather was turning cooler. The sky was as gray as Jeremiah's hair and his mood. He wished Karen wasn't so enthusiastic about his prophet job. She was more gung-ho these days than he was, that was for sure. Love had changed everything for Jeremiah. Falling in love with Karen had thrown the project into conflict. Destroying the world literally meant destroying Karen. Jeremiah was growing more empathetic the more this new love grew in his heart.

Lately Jeremiah had started to think about who all these seven billion people on the planet were, these people he'd be responsible for extinguishing. The thought of tribes in the Amazon who weren't causing any trouble, living in harmony with nature – did they deserve asteroids being hurled at them from space? How about a Vietnamese bartender, just trying to make his way in the world while providing a little kindness for his neighborhood? Meteors on his head? How about a single mom in Kansas trying to teach her child right from wrong while on the run from her ex-husband who is threatening to kill her? What good would ending her life in a world-wide cataclysm do anyone? What right did he have? And what about all the innocent creatures: the fishes, the birds, the monkeys and the thousands of other species?

Jeremiah had thought through hundreds of distressing scenarios and now he wasn't sure ending the world was the best plan. *Sure people could be kinder to one another, but for the most part it wasn't the humble people that caused most problems on planet Earth, it was the rich and powerful, the elite, the banks and the multinational corporations.* Jeremiah wondered if there was some way he could just get rid of the troublemakers and let everyone else continue life unharmed.

That night, over glasses of water turned to ice cold beers in an IPA style, Jeremiah discussed his misgivings with Karen. Karen started to protest but Jeremiah asked her to hold on and hear him out. He talked about the humble, the meek, the underclasses, the impoverished, with a passion that surprised even himself. Karen listened with her heart. She was so proud of Jeremiah and the burden that he carried, but this outpouring of love for the common people really moved her.

"Oh, Jeremiah, what should you do?" Karen saw exactly what Jeremiah was getting at, and her enthusiasm for the world to end in a burning cataclysm started to wane.

"I don't know, I really don't know."

The two talked late into the night. They prayed together about the problem but The Man Upstairs was quiet and didn't answer. Karen suggested they not go out and preach the next day. Jeremiah agreed, that sounded like a fine idea.

31

Freight Train Of Death

Unbeknownst to Jeremiah and Karen, a series of collisions had recently happened in the asteroid belt between Mars and Jupiter. The collisions had altered the course of a large number of huge space rocks and now a mass of boulders were on a new trajectory that would crash them into the planet Earth on May 25th, sometime around noon, West Coast time. An amateur astronomer in Chile was the first one to notice the asteroids, computed their future path and discovered they would cross the Earth's orbit. He alerted the press, his government, NASA and anyone who would listen. The amateur astronomer's finding were quickly confirmed.

The configuration of asteroids was over fifty miles long and many of the rocks were the size of small skyscrapers. It was a freight train of death and destruction, a catastrophic, life-destroying payload many times worse then the asteroid that killed off the dinosaurs millions of years earlier. There was, literally, no way to hide from the coming destruction. It didn't take long for the news of the coming end of the world to spread through the media to the public. As would be expected, world-wide panic ensued.

Now that May 25th wasn't just a hypothetical date of destruction and was realized as an actual threat, Nathan Dynasty didn't want an underground bunker anymore, he wanted to get off this planet – he wanted a spaceship. He got seven. They were large, nuclear-powered cruisers that could carry over fifty passengers each anywhere in the solar system with enough supplies to last over three years.

His spaceships were built by one of the many corporations he owned through Black Shield. The company, Space Tomorrow, Inc., operated out of a top-secret facility in Alberta, Canada. It wasn't listed on the stock exchange and operated below the radar of the rest of the aerospace industry. It also operated below ground and had a gigantic underground facility where it built the spaceships. The fleet of seven cruisers was currently parked on the far-side of the moon, out of view of the international space community.

There were just a few problems with Nathan's escape plan. Where to go when he left Earth was one problem. The rest of the solar system was notoriously uninhabitable. And then there was the three year time limit. Of course, if Nathan only took a few people with him they would have supplies to survive much longer, up to thirty years or so. But what kind of life was that, floating through the vastness of space until you died with nothing to do, nothing to accomplish? Nathan thought through these ideas, and that didn't sound like the life he planned on living, but it was better than dying in a storm of asteroids, fire and destruction, wasn't it?

Nathan's backup plan – underground bunkers – was the plan he shared with his elite friends, various heads of state and his family. He kept quiet about the spaceships. To anyone paying attention to Nathan Dynasty, they would have seen the world's newest and foremost salesman of underground bunkers. Nathan seemed to be all about the safety of his specially built pleasure houses hundreds of feet underground, built by his corporation, Safe Homes, Inc.

Because every disaster always had a golden lining for people

like Nathan, he made a ton of money selling bunkers to the rich
and famous, the movers and shakers, the heads of governments,
Saudi princes and anyone else who could afford to pay, up front, *in
gold*. Nathan planned on filling at least one of the space cruisers
with gold. Weekly, discreet space shuttle flights started to take off
from Alberta headed to the far side of the moon, packed with gold.

32

Zero Hour

Jeremiah's street preaching gig changed quite a bit after news about the coming asteroid destruction hit the public. People were listening to his preaching now, with crowds up to fifty deep at times. Jeremiah had become a prayer leader, exhorting the crowds to pray to The Almighty for salvation.

Soon there were articles about Jeremiah in the newspaper, about how he had accurately predicted the end of the world for several years. There were photos of the writing on the side of his prophet cart with the number of days left. Witnesses had come forward to verify Jeremiah's authenticity.

Jeremiah was invited onto a late night talk show where he transformed a glass of ice water into a high-quality IPA beer in front of a studio audience. The host took a sip of the beer and said it the best beer he had ever tasted. Jeremiah became famous overnight. The Pope declared him to be a living saint. He was invited to the White House and to speak before congress. He hired a press secretary, an industry legend named Troy Lamont. Jeremiah married Karen in a private ceremony at the White House, officiated by the President. He was on the cover of *Time* and *Rolling Stone* magazines during the same week.

The wide-spread panic that had first ensued had settled down to a low-simmering panic as people had to go about the regular activities of living life until they died in a hail of asteroids. Because people are prone to need a savior, many people started to refer to Jeremiah as the new Savior, the new Messiah, come to save the world in its moment of need. A new religion had sprung up, seemingly overnight, called the Church of Jeremiah.

At least twenty percent of the population were in denial of the coming destruction, Zero Hour as it was being called in the mainstream news. Another fifty percent were aware of Zero Hour, but had accepted their fate, not happily, but they accepted it. The rest of the population of the world reacted in a variety of ways: turning to religions, suicide, reckless behaviors of all kinds, joining the Church of Jeremiah, buying underground bunkers, and so on. While most people were willing to hunker down and let the end come, some people were determined to turn the world upside down before Zero Hour.

Jacques Lapin was one of those that wanted to turn it upside down. He went on a bombing campaign against his old nemesis, the banks, and the Dynasty family in particular. He wanted to have the satisfaction, before the end came, of watching the bankers die, of crashing the world-wide economy, of striking terror in the hearts of those that had caused so much suffering in this world. It was quite a bucket list.

The panic caused by Zero Hour had already had a huge impact on the world-wide economy. Priorities changed, long term goals eliminated and immediate concerns became primary in importance. Many corporation's business models became obsolete overnight. Companies crashed and burned. Millions of people around the world were displaced from their former lives, massive refugee camps arose as thousands upon thousands were pushed to the edge of starvation. Even the economies of the largest, most prosperous nations were effected, shaken to their core. When prominent bankers started blowing up every few days, it pushed the situation past its tipping point.

Nathan narrowly escaped death when a car bomb blew up his chauffeur and destroyed one of his garages and fifteen of his favorite cars. Nathan retreated to his underground bunker while his security detail was increased and international terrorism law enforcement personnel were put on the highest level of alert.

Nathan's bunker was the most elite of any bunker anywhere on the planet. To get to Nathan's bunker one first had to fly to a remote island in the Caribbean, Dynasty Island. Once one had flown by helicopter to this island, one would check in at the fabulously outfitted five-story Hotel Dynasty. Hotel Dynasty was where the super-elite one percent of the one percent went to vacation in over-the-top style. But the Hotel Dynasty was just the capstone of a massive underground pyramid that covered five square miles at its lowest level, one mile under the Atlantic Ocean.

The underground bunker was nuclear powered and was, by any standard, one of the great wonders of the planet. The fact that its construction and operation were nearly unknown to the rest of the world was, itself, another wonder of the modern age. The bunker could house over five thousand people in perfect comfort for as long as needed and was built to withstand a direct nuclear attack. Unfortunately, Nathan's top engineers reported to him that the bunker had only a seventy percent chance of surviving the asteroid strike, and pretty much zero chance if one of the larger pieces made a direct hit on Hotel Dynasty. Nathan didn't tell people this as he sold apartments in his underground bunker to the cream of society. Nathan insisted people pay in gold, of course.

33

Bending More Than Spoons

In the top drawer of his desk Aristotle had a pamphlet from Safe Homes, Inc. He had been buying gold coins to purchase a bunker apartment but the gold market had gone crazy. Usually he was the person who knew what to do before other people because of his vast psychic powers, but this time he was playing catch up. He only needed a small apartment beneath the Hotel Dynasty for himself and Jose, but he wasn't even close to the purchase price yet. He was still getting reports from Claude Lyons. Claude was having dreams lately about a world reborn. Claude insisted that he was sure nothing was going to happen on May 25th. Aristotle wasn't sure if Claude was foreseeing accurately or just in denial like so many other people.

Claude's dreams were about more than just a world reborn, it was a world cleaned up and reordered without the influence of greed or tainted by the presence of bankers, royalty, and especially the Dynasty family. Not that Claude had any personal beef with bankers or royalty, but that's what he saw in his dreams and that's what he reported to Aristotle. Claude was not in the least bit worried about May 25th anymore. He was planning to have his kids over that day for a barbecue.

Claude was not impressed by the Church of Jeremiah. He doubted the world needed a new savior. *People just need to treat each other with respect,* is what Claude thought, *that would fix most problems.* He had watched Jeremiah on TV turn water into beer. Claude was kind of envious. *That's a good trick,* thought Claude as he took a sip from his whiskey sour.

Watching Jeremiah made Claude think about his useless ability to bend spoons and a new idea popped into his head. For the first time he'd try to bend something other than spoons. That night, while playing around in his garage with a piece of sheet metal, he thought about his wife who had passed away years earlier. He could still remember her pretty face in detail. He concentrated on the sheet metal and it started to bend and crease. After fifteen minutes of concentration he was exhausted but the metal had molded into the face of his wife, in 3D. It wasn't a perfect likeness, but close. Claude was amazed about this new twist in his abilities. If he had only thought to try this thirty years ago what a different life he would have had.

Claude started to spend a lot of time working on his new skill and his ability to concentrate for longer periods of time with less fatigue increased. He would finish a can of soda and within a couple minutes he would transform the can into any image he could clearly picture in his mind. His mental abilities seemed to work on any kind of metal, from aluminum to gold, but sheets of steel seemed to work the best.

Soon Claude's little house in San Pedro was getting filled with small metal sculptures made from soda cans, and portraits of famous people made of sheet metal. If this had been a different time and the art market still existed, which it didn't since the panic set in, his work would have made a great gallery show. Without a doubt his pieces would have sold out. As it was, Claude's garage and house became increasingly crowded with his prolific output.

Claude mailed a small sculpture to Aristotle. The sculpture was made from a soda can and the image was Aristotle, standing, wearing his robes. It was a near perfect likeness in miniature. Aristotle was thrilled when he got the sculpture a few days later and he had Maria Montello get Claude on the phone right away. He wanted to know all about what he was holding in his hands. He had no idea Claude had sculpted it with his mind, he was just so impressed by the folk-art quality and the likeness.

An hour and a half later Jose had picked up Aristotle and the two of them were on their way to San Pedro, to visit Claude. After talking on the phone Aristotle absolutely had to see Claude's work, immediately, if not sooner. He wanted a portrait of himself with Jose, if that could be arranged. Claude did his best to tidy up his place, but gave up and made himself a whiskey sour while he waited for his boss to arrive.

34

Joe's Christmas Miracle

L *ove is not supposed to be complicated*, Joe thought. But lately it had become very complicated. It was getting close to Christmas and the world was going crazier than usual. This was, of course, the last Christmas anyone, except possibly Claude Lyons, expected to celebrate. Money was being spent liberally.

All the newspapers had taken to adding the count down to Zero Hour on the top of their front page. *The Los Angeles Times* used a photo each day that looked like the sign on Jeremiah's prophet cart. Today's photo said, "171 days until the end of the world", it was early December and Cindi was three months pregnant.

Joe had been working at Vons as a clerk, stocking the shelves for nearly three months and was starting to feel like he fit in. He had found the one other Bruce Springsteen fan who worked on the night shift with him and they had started to bond over their shared appreciation of the Boss.

Jimmy Cruz was from New Jersey, a second-generation American and very proud of it. His grandparents had come from Puerto Rico and the family had risen from poverty to a small, middle class clan that occupied houses on several streets in Asbury Park, New Jersey. Of course Jimmy was a Bruce fan.

Jimmy had ridden his motorcycle from New Jersey to Long Beach the previous year to be near his son, who lived here with Jimmy's ex-girlfriend. Jimmy worked for sixteen years in strip clubs all over the East Coast, and had a ballsy, no-bullshit attitude with a big heart. Joe liked that about him. *Born in the USA* was Jimmy's favorite Bruce Springsteen album.

Joe showed Jimmy a picture of Cindi on his phone one night while they were working.

"That girl is hot, innocent looking but hot," commented Jimmy with a sly wink, "you better hang onto that one."

"How about this girl?" asked Joe showing Jimmy a picture of Cheryl.

"Not even in the same league, my friend," said Jimmy.

"That lady I wouldn't trust one bit," said Jimmy when Joe showed him a picture of Tracy, "she looks like an evil woman and I've known some evil women in my day."

"I think you pretty much nailed it," replied Joe. The three women had made his last three months miserable, especially the combination of Tracy and Cheryl.

Three months earlier the dinner at Gallagher's had progressed into drinks at Tracy's nearby apartment. The night had turned very drunken and ended up in a threesome. Joe blacked out at some point and woke up the next morning in a strange bed and he couldn't quite remember how he had got there. That set off a whole avalanche of events Joe would have avoided if he had any choice in the matter. Instead he felt like he was being pushed around by forces beyond his control, and one of those forces was a negative-feedback loop called Tracy and Cheryl.

Tracy attached herself to Joe like a leech. She turned out to be a needy person with a narcissistic personality disorder. Cheryl was nearly as self-centered as Tracy. Even though she was lacking the leech-like quality Tracy had, she had taken to calling Joe all the time about the various dramas in her life, and to her, all of life was a drama. Tracy, who was a trust-fund child, seemed to have nothing to do but spend all her time with Joe, and daily she inserted herself into Joe's life. It took Joe just a week to be thoroughly tired of the Tracy and Cheryl show. *No amount of drunken sex was worth this*, thought Joe and he figured he'd just say good bye and that would be that. Joe was so wrong.

Trying to say good bye only made things worse. Tracy upped her game, and turned jealous and possessive. Tracy and Cheryl got in a big fight one night over Joe, and over the next few days both of them would call Joe repeatedly to involve him in their drama. During this time, Cindi hadn't called him once.

When Cindi did call, it was three weeks later, and she was only calling him to tell him that she was pregnant. She had missed her period and then she had taken a pregnancy test. It was positive and Joe was the only possible father. Joe didn't know what to say. Cindi said she wasn't looking for a boyfriend or a husband, but she wanted Joe to be there for the child. Joe promised to be there for the baby, whatever that required. The phone call ended after ten minutes and Joe hadn't mentioned Tracy or Cheryl. When he got off the phone he wondered why Cindi had grown so cold.

Joe thought when he told Tracy about Cindi and his future child that would make it easier to break it off. Joe was so wrong. Tracy not only said that she'd stick by Joe though this, but that she wanted a baby too. And she wanted to get married, before the end of the world.

Joe grew desperate to break it off with Tracy and turned to Jimmy for advice.

"Tell her you're done, period. No ifs, ands, or buts. But a true leech, oh man, I don't envy you one bit, my friend. This isn't going to be easy," Jimmy was sympathetic but really no help.

Nothing worked for two months. Cheryl stopped calling after a while while Tracy held fast. Joe tried to break up with Tracy six times, but each time Tracy won the argument, and the relationship continued until December 15th, the day of Joe's Christmas Miracle.

The Christmas Miracle, as Joe later called it, began quite simply. Tracy called to say she was going Christmas shopping and didn't call back the rest of the day. Nor did she call the next day. When Tracy called the following day she was cold and abrupt.

"I want to break-up," began Tracy.

"What?" Joe was confused.

"No use arguing about it Joe, I've made up my mind," Tracy sounded determined.

"Well, okay, if that's the way you feel about it," Joe was so relieved.

The phone call continued for about fifteen minutes. Joe was, naturally, curious about why she was dumping him. It turned out that Tracy had met some guy named Gary and the shopping story was just an excuse for an afternoon date with him. Now her and Gary were practically engaged. Joe didn't quite get all the details but when he hung up the phone he was wondering if this was the same Gary that Cindi had dated months earlier, not that it mattered. Joe felt a great burden roll off of his shoulders. The leech was gone!

35

Tramps Like Us

Cindi had begun to adjust to pregnant life. The first trimester had not been difficult at all – there was a bit of morning sickness and her appetite had changed and her belly was barely starting to show. Inside her a fetus had formed and the doctor said it had a strong heart beat. Cindi was thinking over names for her baby. She was still a month away from her ultra-sound to see if the baby was a boy or a girl.

Cindi was thrilled to be having a baby, even if she had to do it alone. There had never been a moment when Cindi had even considered having an abortion, and giving up this child for adoption was out of the question. Mike and Leslie had already offered to adopt the baby when it was born, but Cindi told them, "no, but thank you". While her parents wanted the best for her and their future grandchild, they really wished Joe was in the picture.

As far as Cindi knew, Joe was involved with some girl named Tracy. She had heard the news through Ricky and Suze. While Cindi had stopped going to the Thursday night happy hours, the bike people still kept in contact with her. Joe had shown up with Tracy several times at Happy Hour and no one had been impressed.

As for Gary, she finally dumped him for good a week after returning from the desert with Joe. She had been spending a lot of time trying to sort out her thinking and the more she thought about Joe the more fondly she felt about his face. Because Joe had professed his love she thought she had time, but apparently not. After hearing about this Tracy girl his profession of love seemed lacking in sincerity.

"I think the bitch is a psychopath," Suze had told Cindi one night in November while on the phone.

"Really? Do you think Joe actually likes her?"

"I don't think so. Sometimes, when she's hanging on his shoulder he has a desperate look on his face. You know, she hangs all over him," Suze was trying to be helpful, "I think she's really possessive."

"I can't picture Joe with a girl like that," replied Cindi.

Suze sent a photo over to Cindi by text message that showed Joe sitting with Tracy from the previous week's happy hour to help her picture it.

"She's twenty-four and from Newport Beach, in the OC," offered Suze, "she's easy to find out information from because all she talks about is herself."

"Joe looks pretty happy in the photo," replied Cindi, half-listening to Suze while studying the photo of Joe and Tracy. She didn't like the look of this Tracy girl, and was that just a fake smile on Joe's face? She hoped so.

Suze called again one night while Cindi was watching the news on TV. Suze and Cindi hadn't talked in over a month. It was nearly Christmas and by now, the coming end of the planet had become yesterday's news. In the news was that there had been another school shooting, during a holiday pageant, with a dozen kids dead. The newscaster seemed neither surprised or troubled by the shooting. Cindi turned off the TV to talk to Suze.

"How's the baby coming along?" asked Suze.

"Good, healthy," answered Cindi.

"Is it going to be a girl or a boy?"

"I won't know for at least a month," replied Cindi. She had a feeling Suze hadn't just called to talk about her pregnancy.

"So... guess who showed up, by himself, on Thursday?" Suze voice had a hint of excitement, "Joe!" she said, not waiting for Cindi to reply.

"I talked with him for an hour and got the four-one-one. Do you know what he called Tracy? The Leech," Suze burst out laughing, "The Leech," she repeated after a moment.

"The Leech?" questioned Cindi, confused.

"Yeah, the Leech, you know, because she stuck to him like a leech. He misses you, he said so several times."

"Really? I kind of miss him," Cindi still wasn't sure about a relationship yet but Joe was a really nice guy and she had lost him once already. Maybe dating her baby's daddy might not be such a bad idea. Suze mentioned that the Thursday night group were going to have a New Year's party, Joe had said he was going to try and make it, and wouldn't that be a good way to start off the last year on planet Earth? Cindi said she would try and make it too, it depended on her schedule at work.

After getting off the phone Cindi put on Bruce Springsteen's album, *Darkness On The Edge Of Town*, and sat in the low light of the living room listening to the CD. She really wished she could smoke a joint, but all smoking was out of the question until the baby was born. She thought about Shane and what a creep he had been. In spite of the hurt, it was time to start healing. She didn't want Shane to steal any more time from her life. Cindi decided she wasn't going to hold back anymore. If Joe wanted to start dating her, well all right then, she was ready. As the album neared its last song, the title track, Cindi impulsively texted Joe, "Maybe we were born to run." Joe responded immediately, "tramps like us :)."

Cindi called Joe and the two spent the next hour talking on the phone. Cindi explained why she had been so confusing and Joe explained about Tracy the Leech, leaving out a few details like the first drunken night's threesome. The conversation was emotional, like a make-up phone call even though the two hadn't ever broken up. Halfway through the conversation Cindi realized she really did love this guy, and once she realized it she wondered why she had held back because her emotions flowed freely once more and it felt good.

Joe hesitated from saying "I love you," as they got ready to hang up the phone. Cindi didn't hold back.

"I love you, Joe Smith," said Cindi, firmly and with conviction.

"I love you, Cindi Wilson," answered Joe. Of course, he meant it.

36

Anti-Christ And The Beast

Jeremiah was adjusting to his new found fame and he wasn't liking it too much. He realized how much he enjoyed people not paying attention to him. Anonymity wasn't such a bad thing after all. But that had all ended now and Jeremiah couldn't go anywhere without people wanting to talk to him, wanting a miracle, wanting a blessing, wanting to touch him like he was God himself.

The change had forced Jeremiah to upgrade his living situation. Jeremiah and Karen now lived in a gated community and the days of street preaching were definitely over. Near constant media appearances required him and Karen to continuously jet around the world. Jeremiah was well paid for his many media appearances and by the end of the year Jeremiah was among the most famous faces on the planet. *Time* magazine named him Person of the Year.

Troy Lamont, his new high-dollar personal secretary, was very busy managing Jeremiah's schedule. Recently added to his schedule was an appointment to meet with the reclusive Nathan Dynasty at his Caribbean island resort, the Hotel Dynasty. The meeting was to take place in mid-January, the earliest Troy could fit the richest man on the planet into Jeremiah's crowded schedule.

There was also a new security force watching Jeremiah 24/7. Fame attracted more then a few unhinged personalities, the number of death threats alone were troubling. Jeremiah remarked several times how odd it was that a prophet of The Most High should need a security detail. Troy told him, quite firmly, the security detail was necessary and they were staying. Jeremiah didn't see much point in arguing, even the Pope rode around in a bullet proof car.

The Man Upstairs had checked in with Jeremiah several times since he had become famous, just to let him know He was still around and the plan was continuing to move forward. Jeremiah did his best to intercede on behalf of the seven billion people on the planet. Maybe destroying the planet wasn't the best option, he suggested. God said He'd take it under consideration.

Jacques Lapin watched Jeremiah on TV one night near the end of the year. Jeremiah was constantly on television, so this wasn't Lapin's first time watching Jeremiah, but this time it all clicked. He wondered how he had missed it before. Jeremiah was the Anti-Christ, he was sure of it. He was the false prophet that would lead the world astray. The miracles, the prophecy, it was all so obvious. It was just like Dr. Charles Harmon had predicted in his book *The Late Great World* years earlier. And now, with the asteroids on their way, here came the disaster called Wormwood in the Dr. Harmon's book, when a third of the world would be destroyed. Lapin could see it all so clearly. The only thing missing was the guillotines, but certainly they were coming.

Jacques didn't send death threats, he sent bombs, and Jeremiah became the new target of his bombing campaign. Thanks to Jeremiah's security detail none of the first three bombs came close to exploding. The fourth bomb killed one of his security force.

That one exploded the day before Jeremiah and Karen flew off to Nathan's island. To Jacques, the coming meeting between Jeremiah and Nathan was, obviously, the Anti-Christ meeting the Beast. More prophecy coming true.

The massive suite where Jeremiah and Karen stayed at the Hotel Dynasty was deluxe beyond compare. It was several thousand square feet in size, and had four rooms — each one was grander than a Presidential suite at a five star hotel. The suite had a full time staff of three people to meet every need or whim Jeremiah or Karen might have. The views from the fifth floor of the Hotel Dynasty were, of course, fantastic.

All of the grandeur was lost on Jeremiah. He wasn't there to be pampered. He had a message from The Most High to deliver to Nathan Dynasty, and it wasn't a kind message. The media, who followed Jeremiah around like a puppy, had a handful of top news personalities on hand to cover this meeting between this prophet of God and the richest man on the planet. Nathan's staff had arranged for the media to occupy a bunch of smaller rooms on the first floor and the rooms buzzed with activity and celebrity.

"Good evening ladies and gentleman, I'm reporting tonight from the exclusive Hotel Dynasty in the Caribbean," began the stately Dan Macon with his well-known voice, full of gravity and assurance, "tonight the world waits to find out what will take place during this summit between Nathan Dynasty and Jeremiah." Jeremiah was so famous by this point that all he had to go by was his first name. Everyone knew who Jeremiah was.

The TV screen cut to a montage of video images of the hotel, Dynasty Island, Jeremiah, Nathan, and the world blowing up while Dan Macon continued, "there are just 130 days left until Zero Hour, and the world is looking for answers, not just answers, but a savior. There, I said it, the world is looking for a savior. Could it be Nathan Dynasty? Could it be Jeremiah?"

Jacques Lapin, who was watching Dan Macon on TV at that moment muttered to himself, "see, I knew it." He was building bombs in his latest hide-out in an undisclosed location in the southwest United States. Unfortunately, Jacques was so distracted by the news report that he made a fatal error while wiring a bomb. An explosion ripped through the building killing Jacques and seven people in the Thai restaurant next door. FBI agent Jim Dalton arrived a day later to sift through the building's remains. Dalton found several notes in the rubble that had survived the explosion. The notes appeared to have Jacques' distinctive handwriting, but he'd have to wait for analysis before he knew for sure.

Dr. Charles Harmon had been watching Jeremiah with much curiosity too. He had reached the same conclusions that Jacques had about Jeremiah but no one wanted to listen to what he had to say about the matter.

Due to the deaths of those who had come out against him, most of the civil suits against him had been dropped but Dr. Harmon was still in financial ruin. His wife had divorced him and his reputation was in tatters. The people who used to support him wouldn't return his phone calls. Nearly every Christian bookstore had pulled his books and videos from their shelves. When Dr. Harmon called the local newspaper to see if they would publish an article he had written about Jeremiah, the Anti-Christ, and the asteroids, which he called Wormwood, they politely took his name and phone number and no one called him back. Times had changed and no one was buying what the doctor was selling.

37

Heaven's Rebuke

The meeting with Nathan Dynasty was scheduled for 10:00 AM. Jeremiah got up at dawn to do his Tai Chi exercises and to pray. He knew what he was going to say to Nathan, but he wanted to make sure the Almighty didn't have any last minute changes in the plan. The Man Upstairs always seemed to have Jeremiah headed full steam in one direction before switching things up on him at the last moment. It kept Jeremiah on his toes. Today there were no changes in the plan. Jeremiah was full of fire and brimstone as he headed to meet Nathan.

In spite of his gout and irritable bowel syndrome, Nathan Dynasty appeared to be a refined and pleasant individual. Most people who met Nathan were impressed by his humility. The humility that most people saw was a carefully designed mask that hid the devious and calculating mind that was Nathan Dynasty. Jeremiah was careful not to be fooled by Nathan's mask. He entered Nathan's audience chamber, where over a dozen advisers had been gathered to hear him speak to Nathan. Jeremiah was prepared with the word of God.

Jeremiah stood before Nathan and his advisers and opened his mouth. Out of his mouth came a flow of words in ancient Babylonian, which happen to be the same language they spoke on Estes-Sol. Nathan didn't understand what Jeremiah was saying, but two of his advisers did. They both understood ancient Babylonian and were surprised to hear it spoken in a contemporary fashion. Before they could translate the message for Nathan, Jeremiah provided his own translation.

"Nathan Dynasty, your soul has been weighed on the balance and found wanting. The world and the fate of humanity rests in your hands. Only you can save the world from destruction, and this is what you must do, now. You must dismantle your empire and free the world from your evil schemes. I know your heart, Nathan Dynasty and I know you will not listen today, but tomorrow you will listen." Jeremiah turned and left the audience chamber. He left a stunned silence in his wake.

While Jeremiah had been meeting with Nathan, Karen had been meeting with the media with a new press release from Jeremiah. It included, verbatim, both in ancient Babylonian and English, what Jeremiah had said just minutes earlier to Nathan Dynasty and his advisers. The news of Jeremiah's message to Nathan rapidly spread across the world.

38

A Reckoning

The world-wide response to Jeremiah's message to Nathan Dynasty came quickly and fiercely. For someone like Nathan who tried to stay out of the limelight, the global attention was unsettling. The various heads of governments around the world immediately started to apply tremendous pressure on Nathan to comply with Jeremiah's demands. Dynasty loyalists quickly responded that it was Jeremiah who was holding the world hostage, not Nathan, but their pleas fell of deaf ears.

While most of the mainstream media was owned by Black Shield and the big networks did their best to downplay the news at first, but Nathan Dynasty and the history of the Dynasty family was now the most important story in the world. The networks didn't stay quiet long.

The history of the Dynasty family was not a pleasant one and included rape, incest, genocide, colonialism, fascism, several world wars, the build up of nuclear arsenals, and the manipulation of banks and international finance, and worse. Several old letters outlining the Dynasty plan for global dominance were released to the public by a disgruntled Dynasty insider along with a video of Nathan and his family cheering with glasses of champagne to the memory of Adolph Hitler on his birthday. The video just added more fuel to an international fire that threatened Nathan and the Dynasty family with ruin.

Across the globe people poured out into the streets in protest. Banks were looted in many countries and burnt to the ground. In many large cities traffic came to an absolute standstill from the number of people protesting. Jeremiah's message to Nathan was the first hope people had in months that disaster could be averted and the people of Earth were making their voice heard as plainly as possible. Nathan, for his part, was stalling, while he worked out how to make a financial killing off of this latest turn of events. As I mentioned earlier, every disaster had a golden lining for Nathan, and his mind was conditioned to think that way.

Both Joe and Cindi had taken time off work to join the protest in the streets. Cindi, who had a little baby bump, was doing really well with the pregnancy and had the glow of a happy, expectant mother. Joe was quickly adapting his mind to his coming father-hood. It was a big change, but for Joe it came with a feeling that things were headed in the right direction again. He was watching his dreams come true, one by one. He had the new job, the girl of his dreams and now a baby on the way. If it weren't for the fact that the world was going to end in 129 days, Joe would have been contently enjoying life. But the world was going to end, and now, for the first time there was some hope that could it be averted. Like everyone else, Joe and Cindi were out in the streets making their cry for their future, for their child's future, heard.

One news report stated that this was the largest global protest ever. Over two billion people world-wide had turned out in the streets to demand that Nathan Dynasty surrender to Jeremiah's de-mands. Governments around the globe were shaken by the protests and several, weaker despotic governments with strong ties to the Dynasty family fell overnight. The stock markets, which had already been pounded by the uncertain future, completely collapsed. Overnight trillions of dollars in wealth disappeared. Nathan, who invested heavily in solid gold, was the least effected person by the financial upheaval.

That evening Nathan ate calmly in the Hotel Dynasty's splendid private dining room. No one was protesting on his island, and the world's troubles seemed so far away. He was thinking about all the resources he would be able to buy up cheaply once this whole fiasco blew over. The world's ruin was his gain. And then his personal secretary brought him a piece of bad news. His oldest son, Pierre, had been lynched in France and his dead body dragged through the streets.

Nathan felt nauseous. Then more bad news came. His daughter Isabelle, the apple of his eye, and her husband Rupert had been raped, shot and killed in Malaysia during the protests. Nathan went numb. Then a report came that his second oldest son, Standard, had been pulled from his limousine in Washington D.C. by a murderous mob and no pieces of Standard had been recovered. Nathan felt his heart pound like it was going to break. Still more bad news poured in. Within the hour reports of all five of his sons and his precious daughter being killed in horrible ways hammered Nathan.

Nathan broke down sobbing. He vomited, he shit himself, his guts felt like a train wreck and he started to fall apart mentally, mumbling gibberish and curses directed at Jeremiah. His personal secretary called in medical personnel and Nathan was quickly sedated and moved to the private hospital at the hotel. He had apparently had a heart attack and a small stroke. Nathan's people made sure that none of this got out to the media people hovering around.

When Nathan woke around five that morning he was in a hospital bed with an IV in his arm, heart monitors beeping, an oxygen tube in his nose, and a blood pressure cuff around his right arm. He tried to move his left arm but it wasn't responsive. His thinking was foggy, but he remembered all the bad news and his heart was extremely heavy. His personal secretary was sitting in a chair in the room waiting for Nathan to wake up. The secretary alerted the doctors that Nathan was awake.

More bad news had rolled in since Nathan had collapsed hours earlier. It seemed that the extended Dynasty family was being hunted down like animals across the globe. Already fifteen members of the Dynasty family had been killed over the course of the night. Many family members were flying to Nathan's island at that moment for safety.

The Premier of Russia, the Supreme Leader in China and the President of the United States, known as the Big Three, unilaterally dissolved the Dynasty-held central banks in their countries. Many smaller counties followed the Big Three's lead. The Big Three demanded that Nathan Dynasty step down as head of Black Shield, immediately. The chancellor of Germany threatened Black Shield with anti-trust violations and demanded the corporation be broken into smaller pieces. Many of the Dynasty financial centers had been burned over night and Nathan's empire was in ruins, tattered beyond recognition. The world had literally changed in the last twenty-four hours.

Jeremiah had watched the news and seen the protests across the globe. It didn't make him happy. He knew a lot of suffering would come out of this last twenty-four hours of protesting. Jeremiah had been interviewed by Dan Macon and he issued a plea for calm that went out across all the networks, but it was unheeded by the protesting masses. Many cities were on fire and it seemed like civilization was going down in flames and still the people stayed in the streets, protesting. Jeremiah requested to see Nathan in the morning.

Nathan had documents drawn up and he signed them. He stepped down as chairman of the board and director of Black

Shield. The papers were waiting for Jeremiah when he requested to see Nathan. Nathan wasn't seeing anyone today his staff said, but he was agreeing to Jeremiah's demand and he would dismantle what was left of his ruined empire.

Nathan, lying in his hospital bed, was, as you can imagine, in an awful mood and busy planning revenge. *When I feel better,* he thought, *I'm going to go Alberta and take a space shuttle to my seven space cruisers on the far side of the moon, and then I'm going to nuke every last son-of-a-bitch on the planet.*

39

The Rescue

This was, of course, when the aliens showed up. The fleet from Estes-Sol was months ahead of schedule, thanks to St. John of Sol's excellent navigational skills. The *Constant Wind* and the rest of the fleet had popped out of light speed a week earlier, just outside the solar system. During the last week the fleet had moved past the outer planets and now several hundred spaceships were in orbit around the Earth. From the fleet's perspective in space it looked like the world was on fire and St. John thought that maybe they were too late.

St. George of Anthem stood on the deck of the *Constant Wind* with St. John as reports came in. The communications team had picked up broadcasts from the planet. Soon a news broadcast from the United States of America was being played on the deck's view monitors. The news was replaying the message from Jeremiah to Nathan with his demands shown on screen in both English and ancient Babylonian. St. John read the message on screen in ancient Babylonian. The news cut to a special report from Dan Macon on Dynasty Island.

"This is Dan Macon with a special report from the Caribbean where Nathan Dynasty has just signed documents, effectively resigning as the chairman of Black Shield. The world-wide protests have succeeded in bringing down the wealthiest man on the planet. Nathan Dynasty is not available for comment, but released a statement through his personal secretary. The statement... hold on, please hold on, I'm being interrupted by a special news bulletin." Dan Macon's face disappeared from the screen and was replaced by senior news person Rita Morris.

"This is Rita Morris reporting," started Rita with her trademark opening line, "we interrupt this broadcast to bring you a special report from the White House that concerns every man, woman and child on the planet. NASA has just confirmed reports that two hundred and thirty-two alien spacecrafts are now circling the planet. I repeat, NASA confirms that two hundred and thirty-two spacecraft from unknown origins are now in orbit around our planet. Hold on for a special announcement from the President..."

"Well," said St. John looking at St. George, "there goes the element of surprise. Get your crews ready St. George, we're going in right away."

The mission was simple. Each crew had rehearsed it a hundred times.

"This is a rescue mission and not a sightseeing trip," as St. George had put it.

The computers had done all the hard work and had already programmed the thousands of rescue ships with coordinates, names, personal bio info and more about each target location and what to expect. Each crew member carried a stun device to help recover the "clients", as the crews referred to the people assigned to them. They figured they'd get more than a little resistance during their rescue operations, so their devices would come in handy. Stunned people offer little resistance.

Each crew member also wore a special helmet with goggles that gave them the ability to detect people with Estes-Sol blood in their veins. Estes-Sol immigrants and their descendants would appear blue to the person wearing the goggles. So the simple mission broke down to this: collect every blue person – every client, willing or unwilling, at each target location and transport them to back to the ship for processing. Get in and out as quickly as possible.

"Be safe out there," said St. George as he sent the rescue mission on its way.

Quickly, over five thousand small rescue ships shot out the larger spaceships in orbit with well-practiced precision and headed to the planet below. However, the rescue ships were nearly invisible as each one was the size of a small marble.

Glenda of Hillside and her partner Aaron, also from Hillside, a small village on Estes-Sol, piloted their rescue ship toward the Caribbean ocean and Nathan's private island. Glenda was in command of their ship, *#27B/6*, and its seven person crew. She had hundreds of hours of training under her belt – she was more than competent. Their target location was expected to have several dozen clients, maybe more, so Glenda's ship was being followed by two back-up ships. The group of rescue ships looked like three blue and green glass marbles skipping over the top of the water.

The rescue ships were fantastic constructions of what we would call quantum mechanical engineering. Though they looked like little marbles when they traveled they could expand to the size of a ship that would comfortably fit over twenty-four people. Even while traveling as a small marble, the interior of the ship always looked large and expansive and one would never guess that all this room fit into a tiny sphere you could hold in your hand. Well, you couldn't hold it in your hand due to its weight, but it was that small.

The three ships set down on the front lawn of the Hotel Dynasty and instantly expanded to their resting size, nearly fifty feet across. The security guards from the front of the hotel slowly, hesitantly, made their way toward the strange spheres that had appeared on the lawn.

"Do you see that? What are those?" Agent Miller asked Agent Douglas, the security guards, both ex-CIA men.

"I don't know. Never seen anything like them," answered Agent Douglas.

A second later, not knowing what had hit them, both of them lay on the ground, unable to move or talk. Miller was unconscious. Douglas was stunned but awake – he couldn't move.

Glenda had instructed the crew to go in on stun, hit everything that moved. The crew spread quickly through the hotel. Miller and Douglas were just the first two people lying stunned on the ground, soon the whole hotel was full of people on the floor, unable to move.

The crew searched the hotel unhindered, looking for blue people. The search was thorough, as they moved from room to room, suite by suite. It was a large area to cover and Glenda called in back-up. After the back-up arrived, fifty-seven clients including Dan Macon, were recovered from the hotel.

Aaron discovered Nathan in the hospital wing of the hotel and called for a medical team and they moved Nathan to one of the rescue ships. Nathan protested this treatment and Aaron had to stun him. Several more back-up teams showed up. Fifty-seven was a lot of people at one target location. The newly arrived teams checked the vast underground bunker and eighteen more clients were discovered.

After the crews had spent hours on the island, a half-dozen marbles shot back out over the water. They were headed back to their home ship with seventy-five clients on board. Glenda notified her home ship, *The Expedient*, the operation had been successfully completed and they were coming in.

St. John and St. George stood together on the deck of the *Constant Wind* and listened to the reports coming in about the various rescue operation. 3 clients on board the ships, 7 clients, 16, 24, 73,

156 – the numbers kept on climbing. It took all day, but the final count was 31,652 men, women and children, several hundred more than they expected, but pretty much right on target. St. John broadcast the new hyper-jump coordinates to the fleet, and within moments, all two hundred and thirty-two ships disappeared from orbit around the planet Earth.

40

Terrorists

Hours earlier – Jeremiah was being interviewed by Dan Macon when the Estes-Sol rescue crew had burst through the door of the hall were the interview was being conducted. When Jeremiah saw the rescue crew running around stunning people he immediately assumed it was a terrorist attack. Then he was hit with a stun beam and he watched helplessly from the floor as the terrorists carried off Dan Macon and several other people. Jeremiah hadn't seen Nathan wheeled out by the medical team, and had no idea what had just taken place.

Now, hours after the Estes-Sol rescue crew had left, the stunned feeling started to wear off and people were up and walking around again. Jeremiah went around to the people that hadn't gotten up yet to see if anyone needed medical attention. He was surprised that no one was injured. Everyone had just been knocked out with some kind of device, it seemed.

It was a confusing couple of hours but soon Agents Miller and Douglas had organized the survivors of the attack into search parties to look for other survivors. Many people were found in hiding. There was one non-fatal shooting based on mistaken identity. In a short while all four hundred and three people on the island gathered in the massive hotel movie theater to figure out what had happened and what to do next. The internet wasn't working and neither were cellphones, all the networks had gone quiet. Thanks to the protests, the island was now cut off from the outside world.

One of the helicopter pilots offered to fly to the mainland to get news, and help. That was voted and agreed upon. There was much discussion about who the terrorists had been. Everyone had assumed it was a terrorist attack and it had become the working reality. Several TV crews filmed the proceedings in the theater and interviewed various people about their experiences with an eye towards making a documentary someday about this terrorist attack. Jeremiah was called upon to say a prayer over the assembled gathering. Jeremiah stood up in front of the crowd who looked up at him expectantly.

It took a moment but Jeremiah noticed something interesting. There weren't any Dynasty family members present, not that he could see. It wasn't like he would recognize everyone in the Dynasty clan, but he had seen several groups of the Dynasty family arrive earlier that day, before the attack. Now, none of those people were present.

"Are there any people from the Dynasty family present tonight?" called out Jeremiah from the stage. Not one hand went up. Just as Jeremiah had thought – whoever it was that attacked, they had been after the Dynasty family. He surprised everyone by including Nathan Dynasty in his prayer of blessing, healing and safety.

41

Space Refuge #25051

On board *The Expedient*, Nathan was about to be discharged from the medical bay and into the ship's general population. The medical staff had fixed Nathan up quickly with techniques developed over thousands of years. The aliens from Estes-Sol were immortal, after all, and had taken a long time perfecting the healing arts so they could live their immortality in a constant state of health.

Because Nathan had been processed while he was being treated by the medical staff and not with the rest of the refugees, he was still under the assumption that he was a really special person, the richest man on the planet. He wasn't anymore. And he wasn't on planet Earth anymore. He was just a common space refugee, client number #25051. His client number was now more important than his name. He had been assigned a cabin on the third deck level, section H. He had no idea where that was until a kid stopped to help him. The kid had spent all day running around the various decks and knew exactly where Nathan's cabin was.

In just a few minutes Nathan found his cabin with the kid's help. It was small, more like a cell. It had twin size bunk beds and Nathan hoped he wouldn't have to share his cabin. He climbed up into the top bunk and lay awake listening to the sounds of the massive spaceship. He must have dozed off because a loud buzzer sound woke him up sometime later. A polite female voice came over the loudspeaker in the ceiling of his cabin, "dinner will be served in five minutes in dining room C, followed by a new client presentation for those who are interested, thank you."

Nathan opened the door of his cabin and many people were walking by in the hallway. Everyone in his area seemed to be headed towards dining room C. He joined the people, and headed the same way everyone else was headed. Along the way he talked with a Duke he knew from the Vandenberg Group. The Duke told him he had seen the Queen of Belgium treated like a commoner by the people who ran the ship, it was disgraceful. As a matter of fact, everyone was being treated like commoners. The Duke didn't know what to make of the situation but he assumed Nathan Dynasty would do something about it.

The dinner was unremarkable but the new client presentation after dinner was extremely informative. The people of Estes-Sol had put together a video presentation that explained what was going on right now, narrated by St. John of Sol. Nathan sat watching the presentation with interest, this was, of course, all new information to him. Thousands of years of history was covered as St. John explained how insurance worked on Estes-Sol.

Apparently the ancestors of people like Nathan Dynasty had bought insurance before they left Estes-Sol for the social experiment on Earth. The insurance contracts had assured their safe return to Estes-Sol should any global catastrophic event happen on Earth. Contracts were worth more than life on Estes-Sol, and consequentially the fleet had been sent to satisfy the fine print in the many insurance contracts sold over the years. Nathan felt confident headed to a place that respected contracts. Contracts were part of the life blood of financial dealings. Nathan's mind started to turn to how he could profit off this latest turn of event. He was, as usual, looking for the golden lining, knowing that it would show up, eventually.

42

Out Of Long Beach

The day after the protests Joe and Cindi woke up in Cindi's apartment. So much had happened in the last few days. It was like the world had turned upside down. The internet was gone and cellphone service was down, completely useless. There were only a few TV networks still broadcasting and cable TV was gone too. The ATM machines didn't work. The gas stations quickly ran out of gas. Luckily Cindi had filled up her tank right before the protests began.

Both Vons and Ralphs had been looted and burned during the protest, so neither Joe nor Cindi had a job to return to. Joe prepared his Breakfast Special at Cindi's as they watched the news on one of the few stations broadcasting. From what they could gather from the news, most of the world was in ruin. The financial system was completely wiped out, the stock markets crashed and what remained of the U.S. government was hunkered down in underground bunkers for now.

That afternoon Joe and Cindi made a plan to go to Joshua Tree. Cindi wanted to be with her family, and Joe didn't complain. He wanted to leave the city because it felt like it was a powder keg just waiting to explode. Law enforcement had ceased to exist and there was nothing to stop the street gangs from claiming more territory. The city wasn't a place he wanted to raise his son, or daughter, not now.

Over the next day both Joe and Cindi went over their various possessions to make sure they didn't leave anything important behind. Two days after the protests had ended the two loaded up Cindi's truck with the few things they wanted to take with them to the desert.

Joe brought his record albums with him, including his complete Bruce Springsteen collection. No reason to go post-apocalyptic without the Boss. He also brought his collection of short stories. He wanted his son, or daughter, to read his stories some day, if the Earth survived somehow. Maybe that Jeremiah guy would do something to prevent the coming disaster. Cindi filled the rest of the truck with clothes, shoes and several boxes of books. They brought their bikes. Once they had loaded as much as they could into the truck they took off for Joshua Tree. They assumed Mike and Leslie would be all right, and maybe waiting for them.

The freeways to Joshua Tree were remarkably clear until they got to Riverside. There were a number of abandoned automobiles on the freeway but people had pushed the cars to the shoulder and they didn't cause much trouble for Joe and Cindi. The biggest problem was the number of pedestrians on the freeway. Large numbers of refugees were moving in groups along the freeways causing major traffic jams in places. Cindi slowly weaved through the crowds taking over the freeway, careful not to hit anyone.

Once they got past Riverside the pedestrians on the freeways practically disappeared and the road opened up for a while. Night started to descend while they drove slowly through Beaumont and Banning on Interstate 10. Automobiles had been abandoned all over the 10 and no one had pushed them to the side of the road.

Cindi drove along at fifteen miles an hour trying not to run into any of the abandoned cars.

The long, exhausting day of driving had drained the gas tank and the fuel gauge showed they had only a quarter tank left when they finally got to Highway 62. Cindi didn't comment on the fuel level and kept on driving. Joe vaped in the passenger seat of the truck, careful to blow the smoke out the window so that Cindi wouldn't get any second-hand smoke. Neither Joe nor Cindi talked much while they drove through the night. Both were full of worries and anxieties.

43

Surprising News

It was sometime after eight when Joe and Cindi arrived at her parent's house. The low fuel light was on, but that didn't matter for now. The house was dark but Cindi didn't seem concerned.

"Dad's probably looking at stars in the backyard," commented Cindi as they got out of the truck.

Mike was, indeed, looking at the sky from the backyard. Both he and Leslie were looking at the night sky through Mike's telescope, perplexed. Mike was doing his best to find the freight train of asteroids headed towards Earth, but wasn't having much luck.

Mike wasn't the only astronomer trying to find the incoming asteroids. They weren't on the trajectory that everyone had been watching for months. The asteroids were missing?!

In Siberia, senior astronomer Sergei Mironov had seen what happened to the asteroids. He had watched it all happen through a very large telescope at the Siberian Astronomical Center and recorded it on video. The lead boulder in the freight train had started to crumble and then blew apart in a massive explosion. The explosion started a chain reaction of collisions and explosions among the following boulders and much of the remaining rubble had been flung off into space. Now a collection of harmless small rocks had replaced the freight train of boulders and they were on a new trajectory that would miss the Earth entirely.

Sergei was at a loss to explain the explosions, taking place in the vacuum of space and all. The whole event was completely inexplicable. Sergei and his team of astronomers were working on theories about how this fantastic, yet unexplainable event could have happened. In an odd coincidence, the destruction of the asteroids had come in the same hour Nathan Dynasty had signed the documents stepping down from Black Shield.

Sergei had contacted the Russian Space Agency about the asteroid explosions and disintegration. Slowly the news of the miracle in space spread around the world. Because only a few radio and TV stations were still broadcasting – the power was starting to go out as energy grids around the world collapsed or ran out of fuel to provide electricity – news was traveling slowly.

The news of the space miracle hadn't reached Mike and Leslie in Joshua Tree yet, and Mike was puzzled that he couldn't find the incoming boulders. Just a week earlier he had located them with his telescope and watched them for a while, fascinated by the fifty mile long string of boulders, silently flying through space.

Leslie heard Cindi's truck pull up and then a knock at the door.

"Mike, I think the kids are here," said Leslie as she went to answer the front door.

There were hugs all around. Mike, excited to see Cindi and Joe, quickly rolled up a joint. He had been practicing and this joint was supremely rolled. He lit it and passed it around. Even Joe took a big hit off the joint when it was passed to him. There was much to discuss and the joint quickly loosened up the conversation.

They sat in the living room and talked about the recent events that had transpired so quickly: the protests, Nathan Dynasty stepping down from Black Shield, the world in shambles, and of course, the still incoming asteroids. The TV in the living room was on and tuned to the only station Mike could find still broadcasting, an ABC affiliate out of Palm Springs. News ran continuously with both national news and local interest news – like where to find the nearest refugee camp. A report on the camps in the Coachella Valley was interrupted by a special report the station had just received, and it was about the asteroids. All four people turned towards the television to watch the news.

The special report was from the network and had been beamed out to a satellite link which transmitted it to every ABC affiliate still broadcasting. The report began with Sergei's video of the destruction of the asteroid freight train with a voice over by the news anchorperson.

"Scientists around the world are at a loss to explain what has just happened, but the threat is over, I repeat, the asteroids have been destroyed and the threat is over!"

The footage was quite spectacular and looked like something out of a Star Wars movie. Joe was stunned. He had never seen anything like it and was the first one to speak, "Oh wow," was all he could say. The report continued with charts and computer simulations that showed what had happened to the asteroids. Disaster had miraculously been averted! The report noted that the explosions had occurred in the same hour Nathan Dynasty had stepped down as chairman of Black Shield. The anchor person said it was an amazing coincidence.

The report was followed by a second special report that concerned the strange disappearance of nearly every member of royalty on the planet. The Queen of England had disappeared along with her whole family. Security cameras had captured the whole event. A whole fleet of strange looking spheres had suddenly appeared on the lawn of Buckingham Palace and numerous people from the spheres in black outfits had stormed the place. All over the Palace guards and innocent bystanders were dropping like flies. It looked like a terrorist attack. The news report showed only snippets of the attack before getting to the heart of the issue.

"This is Rita Morris reporting," began the well-known voice of Rita Morris, "the public is stunned today to find out that the Queen of England has disappeared along with her whole family." The video showed heartbroken, sobbing people on the streets of London.

"Reports have poured in from around the world, reports with terrible news. Thousands of these apparent terrorist attacks were carried out immediately after the protests against Nathan Dynasty. Now, around the world, not only the royals, but the entire Dynasty family is missing, completely gone. There is no word of where they have gone or who the attackers were. No terrorist organization has taken credit for the sophisticated attack. Experts are still going over the video evidence of the kidnappings. This has been Rita Morris reporting." Rita's face disappeared from the TV screen and the local news began again.

It was a shocking pair of reports and everyone sat staring at the television for a moment before conversation started back up again.

"We're saved!" stated Mike quite excitedly and there were high-fives all around followed by hugs and tears of joy. Mike disappeared into the kitchen and came back with a bottle of champagne and four glasses. "That's cause for a celebration!"

44

The Blessed One

The helicopter pilots – there were six of them – began the process of moving people from Dynasty Island to a refugee camp on the mainland. The lone helicopter pilot who had originally flown to the mainland for news and help had come back with the surprising news about the missing royals several days later. The royals were gone, all of them and so were the Dynasty family. No one knew who took them, or where they had gone.

Jeremiah knew where they had gone, The Man Upstairs had shown him. He had a vision the previous night of the spaceship fleet. He saw Nathan eating in a large dining room with many famous faces, including Dan Macon and the Queen of Belgium. In the vision The Almighty showed Jeremiah where the fleet of spaceships was headed. He saw the beautiful lands of Estes-Sol. The Solarians had taken remarkably good care of their world, as people do when they live forever.

In his vision Jeremiah was also shown the great, yet humble, St. Peter of Anthem, who was the supreme prophet of Estes-Sol. He was the one The Almighty liked to talk to when he would visit the planet. The Almighty had informed St. Peter about the coming destruction of the planet Earth. St. Peter had informed the Ruling

Council and within months the mighty insurance companies of Estes-Sol had launched the fleet to satisfy their contracts.

After the vision of Estes-Sol The Almighty had thanked Jeremiah for his participation in His plan to rid the world of the corrupting influence of the Nathan Dynasty and the rest of the immigrants from Estes-Sol. The Almighty assured Jeremiah that he could keep the special gifts he had developed, like turning water into beer.

Jeremiah said, "Um, thanks..."

The Man Upstairs said he'd talk to him later, but for now, why didn't he take some time off... and then The Almighty went quiet.

Jeremiah came out of the vision, a little put off by The Almighty's abrupt dismissal after twenty-five years of work. After all, he had been through a lot of crap over those years, it's not like he could easily walk away just like that. He couldn't help but feel like he had been used.

The process of clearing the island to the mainland took several days, even when the National Guard got involved. During that time word came that the asteroids had exploded and the threat was gone. A great relief had begun to sweep across the world and a week after the first protests the people turned to the streets one more time, this time to celebrate.

Jeremiah and Karen had been flown to Washington D.C. and arrived there before the celebration in the streets took place. Everywhere Jeremiah went he was treated with great respect, almost like a deity. Jeremiah insisted that he was just a man, but the reverence grew.

The President and Vice President had disappeared along with the royals. The Speaker of House, Tom Ryan, now out of the undergound bunker where he had been hiding, had been sworn in as President. Tom Ryan invited Jeremiah and Karen to the White House to host an interfaith conference with the Pope. Jeremiah turned Tom Ryan down, not only because he hated Ryan's politics and religious hypocrisy, but he didn't want to be the focus of a religious conference.

Several weeks later Jeremiah's found out he *was* the focus of an upcoming religious conference he had no control over. The Church of Jeremiah were planning a gigantic celebration festival and conference for May 25th. Zero Hour had transformed from a day of fear into a day of celebration across the globe, a day of peace, a day to be remembered forever.

Most members of the Church of Jeremiah worshiped him as a living God. They would set up little altars in their houses and burn candles and incense in front of pictures of Jeremiah. Several stylized graphics had come out in the previous months of the Prophet, including one by Shepard Fairey. Many members had the Shepard Fairey image of Jeremiah on their altar.

The founder of the Church of Jeremiah was a silicon valley CEO name Paul Stakes, a brilliant and well-respected technical genius. Paul Stakes was a descendant of immigrants from Estes-Sol who had arrived a generation earlier. Paul and his family had disappeared along with the royals, the Dynasty family and many of the biggest names on the planet.

The disappearance of Paul had thrown the Church of Jeremiah into disarray for a week but Hans Von Engels, Paul's second-in-command quickly took over the Church. Within a few weeks Hans had assumed the main leadership position of the Church and he had also launched The Life Celebration Festival and Conference for the weekend surrounding May 25th.

Jeremiah had flatly refused to appear at the festival but that didn't deter Hans Von Engels, not one bit. He didn't think Jeremiah was a living God, not really, and he wasn't going to let a mere man get in the way of his festival, even if it was the figurehead of the Church.

Hans circulated a memo written by Paul Stakes before he had disappeared, titled "The Reluctant God" describing the obvious humility of Jeremiah to resist their efforts to deify him. Paul had referred to Jeremiah several times in the memo as "The Blessed One", and as "Savior of The World" more than once. For many of the members of the Church it was like throwing red meat to wolves, and they ate up the memo as further proof of Jeremiah's divinity. The memo was widely circulated and many members called the memo The First Letter of St. Paul.

45

Changes

Aristotle and Jose had joined the Church of Jeremiah. They belonged to the Hollywood chapter and were planning on going to the festival in San Francisco's Golden Gate Park, but it was going to be expensive. Money was pretty much useless now. Due to the general economic collapse people wanted gold, silver and other valuables now, and the people who would still trade in U.S. currency wanted lots of dollars for whatever they were selling. Everywhere barter was becoming the popular way of conducting transactions.

Many multinational corporations were devastated by the events since mid-January. Without the large banking houses international shipping came to a standstill, and quickly all forms of fuel started to become scarce. Food disappeared off of the shelves of any grocery stores still operating. Quickly life was changing and it seemed the modern American way of life was being left in the trash can of history.

People had started to leave the cities – not everyone, but many people. As the weeks went by refrigerators emptied, as did pantries and cupboards. People simply started to run out of food. Because of the collapse of the economy there were no jobs, anywhere. The government ran refugee camps, and they grew to the size of small cities. By the end of February the situation had turned desperate and then a large flu epidemic swept across the United States of America. Thousands of people died including Jose Ibis Esteban St. Marie.

Aristotle had become severly sick from the flu epidemic but survived. His heart was broken and he wished he had died too. He sat on his sofa starring at the portrait of him and Jose made out of sheet metal over the fireplace in his lonely Hollywood home one afternoon. The likeness was remarkable.

Aristotle was drinking the last of his once-extensive gin supply. He missed Jose something awful. He started to cry. Aristotle cried for several hours, on and off. Sometimes he would just make sad snuffling sounds for several minutes, and then he would cry, really bawling for a while. He lay on the sofa holding a pillow. All his makeup had run down his face and he was quite a sight.

He fell asleep on the sofa and had a dream. In his dream he was standing in the bathroom, cutting his hair short. As he cut his hair it would grow back longer and longer. Soon Aristotle was buried by his own hair, suffocating. He woke up with his face buried in the pillow.

Night had fallen when Aristotle got up from the sofa and went into the bathroom. He looked in the mirror at his face with makeup streaks and smears all over it. Aristotle washed off the makeup, and as he dried his face he stood staring at his hair in the mirror. *It sure has gotten long,* he thought. He reached into the drawer in the bathroom vanity and grabbed a pair of scissors. He cut off a long strand of hair. It didn't grow back, and Aristotle smiled at himself. He started cutting more hair. In ten minutes a pile of hair lay in the sink and Aristotle had a short and choppy new hair style.

Aristotle went into his dressing room and changed his clothes. He put on a pair of jeans, a fresh T-shirt, a sweatshirt and comfortable walking shoes. He packed some gold coins, a fresh change of underwear, a deck of tarot cards and a few supplies in a backpack. He went out his front door and locked it. He put his keys under a boulder in his yard. It was late March when Aristotle headed off down the street to join the migrant population out on the highways of the nation. He planned on heading north. He was headed to San Francisco.

46

In Search Of
A Whiskey Sour

As the food started to run out, Claude Lyons, pondered what to do. He didn't have a lot of options. He had lost contact with his family when the phone lines went down. The electricity had gone out weeks earlier and everything in his refrigerator had gone bad. The water from the tap had gone dry. His supply of candles was exhausted and the outlook for staying in San Pedro was growing dimmer every night. His dreams had grown post-apocalyptic. On top of it all that, he hadn't had a whiskey sour in weeks. The thought made him thirsty and his thirst gave him motivation one night to see if he could find a bar somewhere.

Claude left the house with not not much more than his keys, his wallet and the clothes on his back. The street lights were all out, as usual now, and Claude walked by the light of the nearly full moon. He walked down to South Gaffey Street and headed north. Every business along the street was closed so Claude kept walking. He eventually reached the 110 freeway. He headed out onto the freeway, which had become a giant migrant camp.

As Claude walked through the camp he felt like he was walking through one of his recent dreams. He saw a sign on a tent, which said, in crude writing, "Bar". Inside the tent were two people sitting around a small table and a bar was set up in the back of the tent. The bartender was wearing a pair of guns in holsters on his hips.

"No loitering, grandpa," said the bartender. Claude didn't look like a paying customer to him.

"Do you serve whiskey sours?" asked Claude, not to be put off by a gruff bartender.

"Maybe," replied the bartender, "what kind of money do you have?"

Claude pulled a ten-dollar bill out of his wallet and the bartender laughed.

"Do you have nine more of those? Maybe then I'll see if we serve whiskey sours."

Claude didn't have more than thirty dollars with him. He though for a moment and noticed an empty Budweiser can in the trash.

"I'll trade you a small sculpture for a whiskey sour," offered Claude.

"I don't need no sculpture," replied the bartender.

"Mind if I have that can in the trash?" asked Claude, pointing at the Budweiser can. The bartender shrugged.

Claude set the can upside down on the bar. By now the two people sitting at the small table were paying attention. Claude looked at the bartender for a moment and then concentrated on the can. The can started to twist and bend, without Claude touching it. In several minutes the can had transformed into a striking miniature likeness of the bartender, complete with guns.

The bartender picked up the sculpture when it stopped transforming and held it in his hands, turning it slowing around. He was genuinely impressed by the sculpture but really amazed that he had just watched the object transform like magic. It was the most incredible thing he had ever seen. He set the small sculpture carefully on the bar. The two people got up from the table to inspect the object.

"One whiskey sour coming up," said the bartender.

Claude thought the whiskey sour was a little watered down, but he wasn't one to complain. The two other people in the tent bar wanted sculptures too and each of them bought Claude another watered-down whiskey sour in exchange. The bartender had a few more empties in the trash which Claude made into sculptures, once again amazing everyone as the cans crumpled, twisted, folded and transformed as if by magic.

Later, the bartender asked Claude if he had anywhere to sleep that night – a scheme was brewing in his mind. Claude thought about the long walk he had taken to find this bar and what a long walk it would be to go back home.

"No," he said.

The bartender invited Claude to sleep on a spare cot in his tent. He said he'd even make him breakfast if he made a sculpture of his partner, who would be back in the morning. That all sounded just fine to Claude. Earlier, while enjoying his drinks, he thought that he would head towards his daughter's house in the morning and see if any of his family was still around.

In spite of the watered-down whiskey, Claude had a nice content buzz as he drifted off to sleep. During the night he had a dream, and it wasn't a pleasant one. He was being held captive by the bartender and his partner in a cage in the bar tent. The floor was littered with empty beer cans and they were forcing him to make sculptures of the steady stream of paying customers who would pose for Claude. The dream had a greasy and lurid quality.

When Claude woke up from his dream the bartender was snoring on his cot. Claude quietly got up, grabbed his shoes and slipped out of the tent. The moon was still out and lit his way as he walked north up the freeway through the migrant village, up the 110 freeway, towards his daughter's house in Los Angeles.

47

Community

The village of Joshua Tree had pulled together as a community once the world-wide economy collapsed. The vacation rentals stopped immediately, as did the tourist traffic. The only people left in Joshua Tree were the locals. The only traffic on the roads were bicycles and pedestrians. The several thousand members of the community started a food pantry and a free kitchen to make sure everyone was fed. Community gardens were planted and the people who had wells on their land, like Mike and Leslie, allowed anyone with a jug to fill up from their precious water supply.

Mike and Leslie were better off than many people. They had solar power, a well, and an extensive garden already. They shared generously with the community and hosted a number of dinners at their house for their neighbors.

Joe and Cindi had set up in the guest room with the baby crib they had acquired – the room had become crowded. Joe volunteered at the food pantry. He felt better if he kept busy. Daily he would ride his bike down Park Boulevard to the food pantry. Whatever contributions had come in that morning he would stock on the shelf. Most people who picked up something from the food pantry brought something to trade, like chicken eggs or goat's milk or a can of something, like cranberry sauce, from their home pantry. It was amazing how many people had contributed cans of cranberry sauce. Apparently everyone had cans of cranberry sauce sitting uselessly in their pantries.

Cindi was progressing along beautifully with the pregnancy. There were several midwives in the community and Cindi was the focus of their attention. She was getting superior care, maybe better care than she would have under normal circumstances. Because the hospital facilities had closed, Cindi wasn't able to get an ultrasound and was left wondering whether the baby would be a boy or a girl. Joe hoped for a boy, which he wanted to call Joe Jr. Cindi wasn't thrilled by the name but she agreed if Joe would agree to her choice for a girl's name. Cindi's choice was Seraphina.

"Seraphina? It sounds like a snake," had been Joe's response.

"We can call her Sera for short. I really like it, it's exotic," Cindi replied.

"Sera Smith, I could live with that," Joe said, agreeing.

48

A Phoenix

In April the electricity came back on. President Ryan had released millions of barrels of oil from the federal reserves to help kick start the economy. He was in contact with the new heads of Russia and China as well as many smaller nations, and through negotiations and new trade agreements international shipping slowly began to move again, financed by the largest countries in the world. The void left by the disappearance of the Dynasty family and their corrupt economy was slowly being filled by thousands of new companies. New financial systems were being developed and implemented. Soon gas and food deliveries began again. The world that had crashed and burned began to rise from the ashes like a phoenix.

In early May the internet slowly came back to life as power was restored to the grid. On the 10th of May cellphone service came back online. It was a glorious day as phones started to ring across the country.

On May 25th the world celebrated. At noon, West Coast time, the moment when the asteroids would have hit, fireworks were set off around the world. There was dancing in the streets and feasting everywhere. The day was declared an international holiday and a day of peace.

In the guest bedroom at Mike and Leslie's, Cindi was in labor. She had been doing the breathing exercises the midwives had taught her, she hoped it was helping. She had never experienced such pain before. The childbirth was completely natural and no drugs were used – no drugs were available, Cindi sure wished they were. She breathed in and out, she pushed when the midwife said push. She lost track of time. After an especially fierce push, she heard the sound of a baby crying.

"It's a girl," cried a mid-wife.

Seraphina, thought Cindi, she had a weary smile on her face.

After a few minutes cleaning up the newborn, one of the mid-wives placed Seraphina in Cindi's arms. The mid-wife took a picture with her cellphone and then opened the door and walked to the living room where Joe had been waiting with Mike, Leslie and a few neighbors.

"You can come see your daughter now, Joe," said the mid-wife. Everyone started to congratulate him.

"What's her name going to be?" asked one of the neighbors.

"Seraphina," said Joe, "but you can call her Sera." The smile on his face was epic.

49

The Life Celebration
Festival and Conference

In San Francisco, Aristotle had arrived on foot from Southern California for The Life Celebration Festival and Conference. He had bartered his way north with fortune telling and gold coins. Golden Gate Park was set up with many large tents and temporary barriers for the event, there were flags flying and numerous vending booths with people selling food and religious trinkets. The mood was festive and the crowd was large. There was a giant altar set up with a mural of Jeremiah done by Shepard Fairey.

Aristotle wandered through the crowds. After a couple months of traveling to the festival, arriving felt rather flat. He realized he didn't have any reverence for Jeremiah like many of he other festival attendees. It was like a giant family gathering, but someone else's family. Feeling out of place, Aristotle left.

He walked the streets of the city until he came across a used car lot. A Toyota truck with a low price caught Aristotle's eye. Just a while earlier, as he had been walking around the city, he had been thinking about continuing north. *How about driving instead of walking?* he thought as he looked to the Toyota. He went into the small office to barter with the owner of the car lot. In a few hours Aristotle was driving north on the 101, headed to Portland or Seattle, he wasn't sure yet.

50

Light Years Away

Meanwhile, light years away, on board *The Expedient*, Nathan Dynasty was on his way to a new life. It would be another couple months before *The Expedient* would arrive at Estes-Sol. The government on Estes-Sol had built a small city there called Hope for the refugees to live in, quarantined from the rest of the population until they could be considered safe. The Earthlings were bringing a lot of dangerous ideas with them. Many of them would need a complete re-education and that would take years.

Nathan no longer suffered from gout and irritable bowel syndrome, the medical team on the ship had taken care of that with their advanced techniques. He was feeling better than he had in years. On the ship, among the refugees, prestige was now the only currency. Old royal titles were still recognized as were the social status of people like Nathan Dynasty. Once the pecking order had been worked out among the refugees everything had gone splendidly for Nathan. He was busy working out a new banking system for the passengers based on insurance contracts. As always, Nathan was looking for the golden lining, to line his pockets with gold.

Months later, after many hyper-jumps, the ship started to pull into orbit around Estes-Sol. *The Expedient* was worn out from the long journey to Earth and back. Its electronics, its computers, its hull were all on the verge of failing. The many hyper-jumps had strained the ship to the limit.

The navigational computers gave out as the ship tried to slip into its assigned orbit. An explosion took place in one of the engine rooms and the explosions spread. Slowly the mighty ship started to go out of control and head towards the surface of the planet. Amid confusion and terror, the ship began to burn up as it plunged into the atmosphere. *The Expedient*, or the remains of it, were scattered across the Plains of Siren, in the north of Estes-Sol.

Nearly five hundred lives, including Nathan Dynasty, were lost in the accident, the first lives lost on the planet in thousands of years. A planet-wide mourning took place on Estes-Sol soon after the rest of the refugees in the other ships had been safety transported to their new homes in the city called Hope.

After his death, Nathan's consciousness traveled around the cosmos for a while. Reincarnation was a foreign concept on Estes-Sol, so it was out of the question in that part of space. The Almighty hadn't set up life to work that way when He built Estes-Sol. So Nathan, along with the other perished souls from the crash of *The Expedient*, floated in limbo for hundreds of years until his consciousness came across an inhabited planet named Gaia by the natives.

On Gaia people were reincarnated all the time. There Nathan was finally incarnated in a new body, as a baby boy named Nathan Martin. Nathan grew up remembering his past life. He remembered Earth and he remembered his vast financial empire. Nathan got a job in the financial sector of Londinium, one of the richest cities on Gaia. After years spent working for others and accumulating wealth, he finally opened his own investment bank. He hung a sign outside the bank to announce his new business. The sign said Black Shield Bank and Investments. Nathan had plans to conquer the globe and remake his empire as it had been back on Earth.

51

Happily Ever After

After a year or so things returned to normal on planet Earth, but it was a new normal. Billions of people had been displaced by the protests and the ensuing global collapse. Many nations were completely reshaped by mass migrations of whole populations. The flu and other diseases had wiped out millions of people. The possibility of global destruction had changed the thinking of most of the survivors. Every family on the planet had been effected by the upheaval and epidemics.

On Sera's first birthday the Global Conference on Peace was held in Quebec, Canada. It was attended by every head of state from around the globe. Amid great fanfare, a framework was put in place to form a single world government within ten years. The goal was to eliminate world-wide hunger, stabilize the financial markets, eliminate the use of fossil fuels, and promote world peace. The globalization that Nathan Dynasty had spent his life trying to bring about finally took place, a decade after he left the planet. After much discussion the new global nation was simply named Gaia, the ancient greek personification of Earth.

In time, everyone on the planet was free and goodwill between men and women became the common social thread. People dreamed fantastic dreams and their dreams often came true. There was equality and justice for all. The crime rate and unemployment rate were extremely low around the globe. The people of Gaia were strong and industrious and the new companies paid their workers high wages. Home ownership was as common as air. The children were, of course, obedient and loved their parents. And everyone lived happily ever after.

e

Epilogue

Well, not everyone was happy ever after. Here's what unfolded over the next few years.

Dr. Charles Harmon died of a heart attack a week after the Global Conference on Peace. He was last heard ranting about the evil New World Order and guillotines.

Jeremiah didn't hear from The Man Upstairs for nearly ten years, until just after the formation of Gaia. God hasn't said what the plan is yet, but He's put Jeremiah on notice, the vacation is over. Karen is excited to see what's next.

Hans Von Engels and the Church of Jeremiah went underground after Jeremiah retired from public life. Hans told the many members, some who lived on a large commune in Oregon, that Jeremiah would be back someday. The group continued to worship Jeremiah as a living God and awaits his second coming.

Aristotle fell in love with the Northwest and lived in Seattle until he had a series of terrifying dreams about earthquakes destroying the city. After checking the astrological charts, he ran for it and escaped just in time. I won't say much about it because that's a story for another day.

Claude became a world-renowned artist after the art market started up again. His sculptures are in collections throughout the world. More famous than the actual art is his technique. He had become quite a popular TV personality, regularly appearing on talk shows to make sculptures of the host and other guests. By the time Claude died he was wealthy and beloved around the planet. He never lost his taste for whiskey sours.

Ricky and Suze stayed in Long Beach through the whole series of events. Ricky is now a city councilman and Suze is a stay at home mom taking care of their two boys. Recently Long Beach declared itself the International Biking Capital of the World.

Steve, Joe's old friend, never did get a chance to visit Joe. He got married to Irene and together they raised four kids in Portland, Oregon. Joe and Steve kept in touch by phone and keep making plans to get together.

Joe and Cindi were married by a shaman in Joshua Tree a few months after Sera's first birthday. It was a beautiful wedding ceremony. Joe started working at the Stater Brothers in Yucca Valley when the economy took off again. The couple bought a house in Joshua Tree a year later near Mike and Leslie. It has a fantastic view.

Joe ended up publishing several books of his short stories which were mildly received by the public. Cindi loves Joe's writing. Joe has kept on writing and is working on his first novel.

As for Joe's dream of becoming an astronaut, well, at least he has the girl, the house, and the job. Most of his dreams came true and he has the best kid he could ever hope for.

Sera turned out better than anyone could have imagined: She is magical, she is smart, she has charisma, and she has grown into a beautiful young woman. Naturally, she turned out to be a life-long Bruce Springsteen fan. Of course, it would take a whole other book to tell you all about Sera.

o

Outro

The house lights had gone up in the Long Beach Arena and the E Street Band was rocking the classic *Shout* by the Isley Brothers when Bruce brought the band down to a low pulsating beat.

"Long Beach," shouted Bruce, bringing his voice up at the end of the word "Beach". The crowd went wild with applause. Several more times Bruce shouted out to Long Beach and each time the crowd roared back stronger.

Bruce called out like a preacher at a revival, "I want you to go home, I want you to go home and wake up your family. I want you to get them out of bed in their peeeeeeee-jammas. I want you to wake them up and I want you to go outside. I want you to wake up your neighbors. I want you to wake up your whole neighborhood and I want you to tell them that you, that you, have just seen the heart-stopping, pants-dropping, earth-quaking, hard-rocking, booty-shaking, love-making, history-making... the testifying, death-defying, legendary E Street Band..." the band kicked back into a higher-octane version of *Shout*.

The crowd was dancing, clapping and singing along with every word. Joe and Cindi, out on the floor in the middle of the arena, were dancing along with the crowd. The band continued for another five minutes before bringing the song to a close. The concert had lasted four and a half hours and could have kept on going later into the night. No one would have complained, least of all Joe.

J ON CHRISTOPHER was born and raised in Southern California. He lives with his love of more than 30 years, Tania, in the hi-desert overlooking Joshua Tree National Park. Jon's either writing, creating music, painting or designing books for Traveling Shoes Press – and always spending time with Suki the dog.

This is Jon's fourth novel. His debut novel, *Somewhere Out There In The West* was published in the fall of 2017, quickly followed up by his second novel, *Moving At The Speed Of Time* and his third, *Meanwhile There Were Dragons*. He's currently working on his fifth novel.

OTHER BOOKS FROM TRAVELING SHOES PRESS

Emmy Albertina Bogaerts

Emmy, The Memoir of a Flemish Immigrant

Jon Christopher

Meanwhile There Were Dragons
Somewhere Out There In The West
Moving At The Speed Of Time
Realistic Hallucinations

Jean-Paul L. Garnier

Echo of Creation

Gabriel Hart

Virgins in Reverse & The Intrusion

Mark Leysen

The Klown

Nora Novak

Los Feliz Confidential, A Memoir

TRAVELINGSHOESPRESS.COM